Murder! Murder! Burning Bright

## Also by Jonathan Ross

*The blood running cold (1968)*
*Diminished by death (1968)*
*Dead at first hand (1969)*
*The deadest thing you ever saw (1969)*
*Here lies Nancy Frail (1972)*
*The burning of Billy Toober (1974)*
*I know what it's like to die (1976)*
*A rattling of old bones (1979)*
*Dark blue and dangerous (1981)*
*Death's head (1982)*
*Dead eye (1983)*
*Dropped dead (1984)*
*Burial deferred (1985)*
*Fate accomplished (1987)*
*Sudden departures (1988)*
*A time for dying (1989)*
*Daphne dead and done for (1990)*
*Murder be hanged (1992)*
*The body of a woman (1994)*

## Under the name of John Rossiter

*The murder makers (1970)*
*The deadly green (1970)*
*The victims (1971)*
*A rope for General Dietz (1972)*
*The manipulators (1973)*
*The villains (1974)*
*The golden virgin (1975)*
*The man who came back (1978)*
*Dark flight (1981)*

# MURDER! MURDER! BURNING BRIGHT

### Jonathan Ross

St. Martin's Press ⚏ New York

Library of Congress Cataloging-in-Publication Data

Ross, Jonathan.
    Murder! Murder! burning bright / Jonathan Ross.
        p.   cm.
    ISBN 0-312-15599-9
    I. Title.
PR6068.O835M84   1997
823'.914—dc21                                    97-10025
                                                      CIP

First published in Great Britain by
Constable & Company Ltd

First U.S. Edition: July 1997

10   9   8   7   6   5   4   3   2   1

Tyger! Tyger! burning bright
In the forests of the night,
What immortal hand or eye
Could frame thy fearful symmetry?

William Blake (1757–1827)

# 1

For the young and relatively unblooded PC Sims, parking his patrol car in the shadowed lane outside the perimeter fencing and adjacent to the rear gate of the Castle Caldbeck Wildlife Park in the dead hour of four o'clock on a summer's night, it was a time of tiredness and disgruntlement.

He had had five hours of travelling his Division's share of a sleeping countryside for any sounds or signs of a flock of sheep being unlawfully culled. It was a time when he wished seriously that all sheep were equipped with a predator's teeth and an easily aroused irascibility. He had neither heard nor seen anything on his specified ten-minute stops for what amounted to a blind surveillance of black-as-midnight spread-out grazing fields. After four nights of this 10 p.m. to 6 a.m. duty, it seemed to him that he was little more than a bloody useless night-time mobile shepherd.

It was a sweet night, a starlit night of unappreciated earthy smells and night-blooming scents as Sims, standing in the lane and smoking a cigarette, listened in to the darkness for any sounds of distant panicking sheep. What he did hear from behind him were the coughing grunts of lions and the deep rumbling and splashing sounds of what he thought might be the internal workings of a couple of elephant- or rhinoceros-sized stomachs. There were other animal noises, quiet and not disturbing the night or Sims's listening attuned primarily to the bleating of frightened sheep.

With his ten minutes of concentrated listening finished, Sims dropped his unfinished cigarette to the ground with a wish that he could give them up, trod it to extinction and climbed back into his car. Belting himself in and about to turn on the ignition, he paused as he identified the muted sound of a slowly driven vehicle approaching from within the park.

When it reached the gate set in the high wire mesh fencing and was braked to a standstill, Sims could discern the dim glow of its sidelights. In the pause that followed he heard soft footfalls and then the metallic clinking of the gate being unlocked and opened over the sound of the vehicle's idling engine.

With the emergence of a deeply shadowed figure which appeared to be checking the possibility of driving from the park, Sims switched on his sidelights to indicate his presence, preparing to move from blocking the lane. Then, not quite comprehending, he saw the undefined figure – it could have been either male or female – react to the sudden showing of his lights by turning abruptly and retreating back through the gate, the rapid footfalls of its flight cut short by an almost immediate silence.

Sims, taken by surprise and having to unbelt himself, scrambled tardily from his seat and ran to the gate behind which still waited the car with its quietly ticking-over engine. With nothing but the unrelieved blackness of the park's interior facing him he conceded a sort of defeat. He had obviously, he thought, surprised a theft in being of a car belonging to somebody living in the park; a thief who appeared to have held a key to the gate.

Retrieving the flashlight he had disregarded in his haste from his car, he returned to what he could now see was a dark blue Ford Escort. Reaching through its still open driver's door and switching off the engine, he searched for identifying documents. Finding them in the glove compartment, he saw that the car was registered in the name of Henry Fowler with the address 2 Castle Cottages, Caldbeck; this was supported by accompanying papers.

Starting a search of the car before reporting in to Control Room and finding the boot locked, he removed the key from the car's ignition and used it to open the lid. The narrow beam of his flashlight illuminated horribly the bloodied and twisted mask of a woman's staring face and the bloody mash of the side of a man's head in a grisly tangling of arms and legs. Startled, feeling the blood leaving the flesh of his face, he slammed down the lid and stumbled to the side of the car, where he spluttered a horrified 'B-Bloody hell!' as he vomited his supper over his shoes.

Afterwards, cursing what he saw as his stomach's weakness and opening the boot, he forced himself to press a finger and thumb on the pulseless wrists of the two cold hands he could recognize as male and female without having to look at the shattered mess of the man's head or at the dreadful expression on the woman's tortured face staring up at him.

Closing the lid again, he called through to Headquarters Control Room on his car's radio, ordering his voice to the unshaken steadiness befitting an experienced police officer of five years' standing who had happened on a couple of murdered bodies and was taking them in his stride.

## 2

Detective Superintendent George Rogers, dragged by his detested telephone from a three-hour sleep to an unrefreshed consciousness, was not at his most amiable. A dark four thirty in the morning was always an uncivilized hour for his being anywhere but in bed.

The duty chief inspector at the Abbotsburn Police Headquarters had passed on to him the unwelcome information that two feloniously killed bodies, discovered by a patrolling PC in the boot of a car parked inside the Castle Caldbeck Wildlife Park, were waiting on his instructions. There was little more and Rogers expected none, but enough, pending his own arrival, for him to set in motion the immediate calling out of his second-in-command, Detective Chief Inspector David Lingard, the Scenes of Crime Officer, Detective Sergeant Magnus, the Coroner's Officer armed with coffin shells and body bags, and three DCs for preliminary enquiries. He also instructed that the Assistant Chief Constable (Crime), a patronizing and careerist transferee from another force, be informed; he would, understandably Rogers supposed – and hoped – leave worrying about it at least until after he had breakfasted.

That was the routine of it and now Rogers could take a bleary-eyed shower, shave his overnight stubble and dress in something a little less than frenzied haste. Nobody but Lingard would do anything significant until he got there, and the bodies wouldn't be going anywhere without his say-so. Calm and untroubled progress – outwardly, at least – was the ordering of any violent crime he had to deal with; an uncoordinated galloping to anywhere was the enemy of productive thinking.

Physically, Rogers was six feet and two inches of forty-four-year-old tissue, blood and bone, divorced from a wife who had lubriciously preferred the heavyweight attentions of a bull-necked, hard-drinking and otherwise unemployed rugby player. Rogers, black-haired and swarthily skinned with a thrusting inquisitorial nose, was a formidable male of a quasi-uncompromising nature, his brown eyes ready to darken when meeting with cruelty or brutality. No man for the easy smile, his normal expression was one of professional impassivity, tending rather to the saturnine. Despite his occasional forebodings that he might be struck down in death from some unsuspected frailty of his internal organs, his body was, in fact, racing fit and in good breeding condition.

In the shower, his mind blanked against thinking about the bodies to come, he was ready to be more concerned with his present circumstance and condition. Off duty, he allowed himself a nearly obsessive liking for Angharad Rhys Pritchard, the supremely elegant yacht-owning widow of a then retired Royal Naval Commander, and she now occupied much of his thinking. Angharad, of Rogers's own age, was wonderfully lean, small-breasted and narrow-flanked; dizzyingly attractive in his eyes with her shoulder-length ash-grey hair and dark green eyes in hawkish features. As a non-practising and unchambered barrister she wrote papers on marine insurance, charter and brokerage for the committee of the Club Mouillier l'Ancre of which she was a member.

Living in a Spanish-style villa on the costly heights of Thurnholme Bay, only a few miles from Rogers's Abbotsburn and overlooking her yacht's mooring, she could share little of Rogers's circumstances as a rather overworked policeman. Nevertheless, their relationship was a civilized one of a shared warm affection in which he was allowed occasional access to her bed or, more rarely, a berth in her boat, each having agreed not to tread too possessively on the other's shadow. She played golf with him though she seemed not to be terribly committed to knocking a small white ball over often wet countryside, while he – he thought reasonably – occasionally crewed for her in what he considered to be the discomfort of a dangerously unstable, windswept and soaking wet boat.

That, and the demanding nature of his duties, caused him to often cry off the sailing; this, admittedly being something he had brought on himself, led to Angharad enlisting a fellow member of the club as a crewman in his place. He was a not too old unmarried judge whom she called 'Charlie', more formally known as Sir Charles Acton-Turvell MBE; he sat representing the Queen's Justice on the North-Western Circuit and was damned doubly by Rogers for his propinquity to Angharad and for his unfairly owning a boat of his own.

True, there was never any suggestion of a closer female/male relationship, but their continuing association both worried and irked Rogers. In his darker moments he thought he was about to be rejected as a lover, though almost certainly in the nicest and most elegant manner. It irked him even more that he himself had given up smoking his brace of pipes in deference to Angharad's dislike of his addiction to them. While he dressed himself in his white shirt and sober grey suit – he often likened himself on duty to a cavalierly-inclined rook – he wondered if he could successfully, if deceitfully, conceal his enjoying the euphoria of a secret smoke or two or three when not with her.

In case he was suddenly overcome by intolerable temptation, he would take with him one of his pipes and his pouch of rather stale, but still aromatic, tobacco. He could, he thought, be forgiven a weakness or two.

As he left his small and comfortless apartment, he repeated in his mind a so far routinely unavailing wish that this might be the day when his ex-wife's live-in lover – whose expensive grossness he was, in effect, supporting with half his salary – would be kicked painfully somewhere approximate to his genitals during the muddy and ferocious rugby matches in which he played so brutishly.

## 3

The nine miles of undulating moor through which Rogers motored towards the blanketed-in-darkness coast brought him to the lane bordering on the Castle Caldbeck Wildlife Park. As he braked to a halt close to the gate in the mesh fencing, his car's headlights brought into relief a semicircle of three cars and a van, their parking lights illuminating not too helpfully a fifth vehicle, standing inside the opened gate with its boot lid lifted.

Climbing from his car, he saw what seemed to be a waiting-for-him-to-arrive tableau of enshrouding trees containing within them the elegant and always nonchalant Detective Chief Inspector Lingard, and a uniformed inspector to whose shadowed features he could put the name Hassell. Apart from them was a slim woman in a straight tan skirt and white epauletted shirt standing adjacent to a hitherto unobserved black golf cart, Sergeant Magnus with his photographic and fingerprint processing equipment, and two uniformed PCs, one of whom hovered protectively over two coffin shells and their accompanying body bags. Intruding on the early-morning silence was a dawn chorus of distant unidentifiable animal and bird sounds.

Rogers joined them, superficially genial and not showing any haggardness occasioned by his loss of sleep, though about to question somewhat testily the apparently unauthorized presence of the woman.

Lingard, his second-in-command and the personification of blond-haired elegance modelled by his admiration for the snuff-addicted foppishness of the eighteenth-century rake George Brummell, was a man of patrician appearance with a narrowness of features and the daunting blue eyes of those believed to be *persona grata* with God. Even illuminated only by the cars' indifferent lighting, his dandyism was obvious with his expensively tailored summer suit and, of a comparable elegance, a silk shirt modishly high in the collar and long in the cuffs.

He was also a man who had of necessity to anticipate his senior's thinking from his expression. He said, 'We're more or less under control, George.' He indicated the woman with his head. 'Mrs Wing is the chief security officer for the park. She was told by one of her staff what was happening and she's now been of help in identifying the bodies.'

Rogers, showing his teeth in a greeting, could now see that Mrs Wing, a neatly small woman, was wearing uniform. With her black hair drawn back behind her head, black-pupilled eyes and a generous mouth in a good-looking face – it was high-cheekboned and elfin – she emanated a sexual attraction which was as unsettling to him as it was unwanted at the scene of a double murder on a dark morning. At first sight, she reminded him of a younger Angharad though there was no recognizable physical resemblance.

She said, 'I was told that you would be here,' letting him come towards her to shake her hand which felt surprisingly strong in his own.

Her accent was definitely Cheltenham Ladies' College, touched, he thought, with a little authority. 'I understand you've identified those two in the boot?' he said.

She seemed to look surprised. 'Only possibly. One appears to be Henry Fowler who's one of the keepers . . .'

He stopped her in mid-flight with his upraised hand. 'I'm

13

sorry,' he apologized. 'Do you mind? Let me look at the bodies first with no preconceptions; then, if I may, I'll come back to you.'

He turned, speaking to Lingard. 'While I'm doing that, David, fill me in with what we've got, will you?'

Taking a cableless floodlamp from Inspector Hassell and approaching the open boot of the abandoned car, he switched on the lamp to fill the boot and its grisly contents with an almost sizzling white light. It took him a few seconds to make clear and identify the tangling of twisted arms and legs of the two bodies in there.

The man, so clearly dead, was dressed in a lemon yellow shirt with off-white linen trousers. These were unzipped and showing green-striped boxer shorts. The woman, partly beneath him, had presumably worn a blue spotted lightweight skirt, now removed and lying under one stockingless leg. Her darker blue satin blouse was unbuttoned, revealing a part of one breast.

The man believed to be Henry Fowler had been shot at close range in the side of the head, obviously by pellets from a shotgun. Without moving the badly shattered and bloodied head, Rogers could accept that the closeness of the charge of shot had also caused an exit wound. What was left of the face was void of any expression but that of death.

The woman had met death differently. She had not been shot, but the face, upturned to his gaze, had been battered and imploded into something so nightmarishly dreadful that he knew it would stay with him in his worst dreams. He had no need of an overly suspicious mind to suppose that she and the man had been killed *in flagrante delicto*.

Suppressing his revulsion, Rogers touched the unbloodied flesh of arms and legs, feeling the coming coldness of deaths which must have occurred, at the most, only a few hours earlier. There was pity in him as he did it, though he would not allow it full flow until he had decided that death had come unearned, and not by what he could think of as a divine or natural justice. Too, a Rogers on the job always suffered the unsettling conviction that the victim of a murder would be

14

watching him with reproachful eyes should he not be doing his damnedest to bring the murderer to justice.

'Being dead', he muttered ruminatively and primarily to himself, 'is an unfortunate something that nobody has yet survived to tell me what it's like.' To Lingard, he said, 'Tell me what the circumstances of their finding were, David.'

Lingard, pinching out Macouba snuff from a tiny ivory box and charging his nostrils with it, told him briefly what PC Sims had reported about the flight of the unknown driver of the car and Sims's subsequent finding of the bodies. 'He's waiting now to get back to his sheep-watching detail,' Lingard added. 'A man very worried that his sergeant's going to yell blue murder at him for not having done his quota.'

'No,' Rogers said dismissively. 'He's to return to his station and prepare an immediate and detailed occurrence report to be on my desk before he goes off duty.' He asked, less abruptly, 'And how about your side of it, David?'

'Egad, George, I've been busy doing your chores waiting for you to get here. I've sent DCs Goater and Mallard – as you know, a couple of the dimmer types – to scour the park for anything relevant, ordering them to try and avoid being eaten by the lions. Magnus has done his photographing of the bodies *in situ* and is now waiting for the condensation on the car and the gate lock to pass off so that he can dust for fingerprints. The duty security guard – his name's Bloor and he was trundling around in a golf buggy – arrived here shortly after I had and I sent him off to dig out his chief . . .' – he lowered his voice – '. . . who is the wholly yummy Mrs Wing – Lesley Wing she told me it was. She came here posthaste and I let her see the bodies after due warning that they may not be her cup of tea.'

He inhaled more snuff into his sinuses with what he considered to be a Beau Brummellish flourish. 'Egad! She must be a hard one despite her yumminess. There was none of the old female blenching business or any attack of the vapours you'd expect, and the gallant lass put her nose not unadjacent to the poor woman's bosom to try and identify whatever scent she might be wearing.'

15

'And she knows them both, it seems?' Rogers, thinking that the horrors in the boot seemed justification enough for feeding his nervous system with nicotine, was stuffing tobacco into his neglected pipe and flaring a match at it. Without actually seeing her, he was conscious that Mrs Wing was watching him closely.

Lingard said, 'The dead man is definitely Henry Fowler who's employed here as a keeper. He's said to be single and lives as a lodger in the village close by. The woman is believed to be – well, almost certainly is – Harriet Stoner, the veterinary's secretary employed here. So far as Mrs Wing knows – or so far as she allowed herself to imply – the two weren't known to be having it off on a day-to-day basis.' Lingard was cynical. 'I suppose there could be another reason for chummy being unzipped and the lady skirtless. Incidentally, although Sims said he heard the gate being unlocked, there's now no key in it.'

Rogers reached and pulled down the boot's lid on its dreadful contents, then gave Lingard further instructions which included getting the Major Incident coach and its operational personnel on site and calling out Dr Wilfred Twite, the county's Home Office appointed pathologist; a slapdash anatomist but supremely efficient at finding the means by which his friend and benefactor Death had entered any particular cadaver.

Finally, reluctant to pass on too many tasks to Lingard, he said straightfaced, 'while you are getting on with that, David, I'll force myself as your senior to take over and have words with the apparently edible Mrs Wing.' He thought it was bloody tough being a second-in-command, but that was life at its most exacting and said to be good for the soul. He had been through it himself and survived, so he knew.

With Lingard leaving him – by now there was an oystergrey lightening of the sky on the horizon – Rogers put the disagreeable fact of two dead bodies waiting on his total involvement to one side for the moment and moved to Lesley Wing, now sitting in the golf buggy and talking into the personal radio fitted to it. When she had finished and slid

16

from the buggy, he smiled genially at her and said, 'It's George Rogers and I'm sorry for keeping you waiting. I understand you're in charge of the security staff here?'

'Yes.' She smiled back at him, her eyes black in the darkness not yet gone. 'Actually all four of them.'

Rogers, already attracted by her friendly personality, said, 'It must be something of a nuisance to have a couple of dead bodies found on your particular patch?'

She had aplomb, appearing not too devastated, in fact not moved very much at all. 'It isn't anything we could have anticipated and naturally I'm horrified that it involves two of the park's employees.'

'You mentioned you could identify them, one certain to be Henry Fowler.' Hearing a shrill scream from the near distance, apparently one of unbearable agony, he paused. It sounded uncomfortably like a woman having her throat cut, but as Lesley Wing was patently reading nothing in it he decided it had come from a large bird. He continued as if he had heard nothing. 'And the woman? You believe her to be Harriet Stoner?'

She looked sad. 'Poor girl. No, I'm certain. The hair is hers anyway, though I've not seen the clothes before. Her face . . .' She shuddered. 'It's smashed beyond belief, but it's her; there's no real doubt about it.'

'They've been known to associate?'

She bit at her lower lip. 'I wouldn't like to be definite on that. We're a quite close community here, almost living in one another's pockets, and I think I'd like notice before I said anything derogatory about Harriet.' She looked apologetic. 'Perhaps later after I'd thought about it?'

'I take it that you'd noticed they were both partially unclothed. You were surprised?'

'Damn,' she said softly, almost under her breath. 'It seems you won't take no for an answer.' She seemed as if about to concede something. 'So far as Henry is concerned, yes I was.'

'Tell me who he is, Mrs Wing, and what is he doing here?'

'He's one of the keepers, mainly concerned for the elephants and rhinos. He's not been here very long, but we know him as a very nice man . . . well respected here.'

17

'And Miss Stoner?'

'She's Mrs Stoner. William Stoner's her brother-in-law and she lodges with him in the village.' Her face was giving nothing away and there was little in her words to suggest there might be more in it than just that. 'She's Mr Latouche's secretary and veterinary assistant.'

'And what does Stoner do?' He thought her resemblance to Angharad was going to be unsettling to him and he tried to put the physical aspect of her out of his mind.

'He's a guard.' As expressionlessly as the detective, she added, 'He was on duty until two o'clock this morning.'

'He'd be in bed now?'

'He'd be a fool if he weren't, wouldn't he?'

He grinned at her. 'It's a hard life for some of us, so could you have him dug out and report to me as soon as he's dressed?'

When she nodded her agreement, he said, 'Mr Lingard tells me your chap Bloor is the guard on duty who caught up with him here. He was driving a buggy like yours.'

'That's so.' She was crisp and authoritative. 'He's on the 2 to 10 a.m. night shift. We work three shifts here and operate three carts – one of which is for me – which I believe is a security innovation. They run on batteries, they're silent and virtually invisible at night and we've dropped into the habit of calling them Prowlers. Which isn't their proper name, of course.'

'I can imagine why,' he said approvingly. 'They're what I've been calling golf buggies.' He looked at his wrist-watch. 'I'd like to speak to Bloor before he goes off, so could you make him available?' He liked this woman. She seemed very much a no-nonsense, self-sufficient character, likely to give him a bit of stick at times, though in doing so unlikely to lose any of her dark-haired attraction for him.

'I'll keep him on tap and ready for when you want him.' She hesitated. 'I should warn you . . . no, not warn, but tell you that his imagination does occasionally run riot. And he's certainly over-qualified for the job he's doing.'

'He is?' Her eyes, while not being intrusive, hadn't left his and he thought he could sense the not unwelcome emanation of a woman's interest in him; conscious too that there had been a pause in which he had been staring back at her.

'It seems so,' she replied. 'He has a BA in Humanities and a couple of other subjects, none of which he considers of value in the current market for employment.'

Breaking off contact, he looked past her to the park entrance. 'You know, I imagine, who would hold a key to the gate?' The headlights of the waiting cars were now dulling to a dirty orange with the coming of daylight, though fingers of darkness were still waiting beneath the lushness of the trees.

'I exaggerate a little,' she said, appearing to be slightly amused, 'but mostly everybody employed here who uses or might use the service road. I also hold three in the guardroom, and people like Harry Halcro the head keeper and his staff, Jacques Latouche our resident veterinary, and, of course, Matthew Wilder the general manager. He's not available at the moment, being on a touring holiday in France.'

'So who owns the park and the castle?' He smiled warmly at her, his amiability easily forthcoming for attractive women.

'Toby Wimbush,' she answered him. 'He's away too, though not on holiday. He's in Russia trying to buy up a few wolves. I think,' she added after a short pause. 'He doesn't need to account to us where he's choosing to go.'

'I imagine not. On the other hand, I do have to make my number with whoever's in charge. So who would that be?'

'Mr Wilder normally, but as I'm in charge of security anyway, it's been accepted that any current problems are mine to manage.' She seemed amused. 'That sounds of greater importance than it actually is.'

'I'll be most happy to confine my problems to you in particular, though this one would have been aimed at you anyway. Under what circumstances would Mr Fowler's car be in the park?' In the advancing daylight he could see that her hair really was as black as the night just going.

'Under any circumstance, I imagine. He lives here in the village.'

'The village?'

'It's called the village. There are eleven cottages owned by the park that have always been attached to the ownership of the castle, and they're mostly occupied by park employees. Henry lodged in one of them.'

'I see. I'll need to see his room or whatever.'

'I'll arrange it.'

'Do you know where he comes from? If he has a family? I shall need to have them informed.'

She showed a possible frustration. 'That's something I can't help you with, though I do know he's here as a single man. Wilder holds all staff records and I have no access to them.'

'You wouldn't have Mrs Stoner's previous address, or her brother-in-law's, I suppose?'

She shook her head. 'I have neither.' She hesitated. 'Stoner is one of Toby Wimbush's special concerns. I rather believe he served with him in one of the Royal Marines' Special Units; and Toby owes him. I'm not sure for what, or supposed to even know about it, so treat it in confidence.'

'And Harriet?'

'All I know is that she comes from Crouch Aughton and her husband's name is Laurence, and . . .' – she appeared to become heated – '. . . he's apparently as despicable a man as his brother.'

'There's more, Mrs Wing?' He smiled encouragingly.

'No. Certainly not before I've thought about it.'

'I understand,' he assured her. Then he added, 'In case I have to chase you up sometime, could I ask if you also live in the village?' He was partly working for himself now.

She showed her pink tongue in a laugh. 'I don't believe it's yet an official secret, but I do have an apartment in the castle and not too far away from where my office and guardroom are. It goes with the job as all the administrative work is done in the ground floor of the East Wing.'

Chancing his arm, though feeling gauche in doing so, he asked, 'Does your husband also work in the park?' The off-duty part of his mind prompting the question was wondering whether, were she still married, it would be to some body-beautiful and hairy male with bulging biceps, fast on his feet and owning to a short-fused temper towards another man daring even to think of nudging him to one side.

She shook her head, neither losing her look of amusement nor detaching her steady regard of him. 'There is no husband. Is that what you wanted to know?'

It took him several long seconds to give her his answer, thinking to hell with it, why shouldn't he? 'In a way, yes,' he said, trying to look as if it meant nothing personal to him, 'I did.'

As though to put an end to that subject, she nodded in the direction of the two bodies in the car, now exposed to the growing brightness of the rising sun, asking, 'How long would you say they'd been dead?'

'A few hours, though that's guessing and anathema to a policeman. We'll know more precisely when the pathologist arrives.' He looked again at his wrist-watch. 'If we've found him – and sometimes we can't – he shouldn't be too long. Is there any particular significance in your asking?'

'Only that Stoner could have been the guard on duty when all this happened. Bowler, the guard before him, would have gone off at six last evening.' She paused, searching his eyes, then said, 'When you see me later, would you tell me how those two died? I can guess, but if I know for certain I may be able to help.'

'I'd be obliged were you able to.' He smiled at her. 'I'd be even more obliged if you'd notify all the top brass of the park of what's happened and ask them not, definitely not, to come here before I've finished with the bodies. I'd also like you to close off the entry to this road, again until I've finished with it. Are you happy with that?' God! he thought, how sun-risen daylight was becoming to her attractiveness, though probably diminishing to himself. He thought quite disinterestedly – he convinced himself that he was sure about this – that, if he held her in his arms, her head would reach just below his chin.

'I think I'm going to be. There's not a lot of excitement in organizing security shift duties and making sure that some moron doesn't get an urge to climb in with the lions or to play with the rhinos. I've never been in on a murder case before.'

'So what have you been in on, apart from this?' From the way she had said it, he suspected he was going to be surprised.

21

Somewhat wryly, she said, 'I was a lieutenant in the Corps of Royal Military Police – on the investigational side – made devastatingly redundant in one of the past rounds of service cuts. It was a career I had wanted since I'd graduated.' Despite her words, there was no bitterness in her voice. 'Does that surprise you?'

'Not too much. I'd noticed you called your security office a guardroom. That's very military, of course, and I approve of it.'

'You'll keep me in the picture then?'

'I shall be happy to,' he promised her as she smiled again and turned away.

He watched her climb on to the buggy's seat and glide noiselessly away, giving him a wave that awoke a few degrees of ferment behind his impassiveness.

Returning to the car, now being examined and dusted for fingerprints by Magnus, was anticlimactic for Rogers, despite the overriding importance of the two bodies slowly cooling with the coming of what must be for him a day of being lied to with a so often put-on wide-eyed innocence.

4

Dr Wilfred Twite's gravel-scattering arrival at the now sunlit scene of the bloody entombments in his white shark-nosed Citroën Safari – an elderly and aristocratic car Rogers had long lusted after, but could never convince himself he could afford – had in it all the elements of a hurried impatience.

Twite was a cheerfully fat and gently sweating man in a lightweight twill suit that did little to conceal a gourmand's huge stomach; this, surely, needed to be held in check by the male's equivalent of a corset. His tightly waved black hair, matching sidewhiskers and Mexican-style moustache seemed more suited to an overnourished man of South American extraction, which he was not. His hands were pale and pudgy

22

and as skilful wielding a scalpel and bone saw as with a knife and fork. That he was gregariously inclined and preyed on married women was only made acceptable in Rogers's eyes – no prig himself – by the reported enthusiasm of the women themselves to be seduced by this most physically unlikely of lovers and by its being none of the detective's business anyway.

Being met by Rogers, Twite climbed weightily from his car, carrying his small black bag which was as likely to contain enough smoked salmon sandwiches to sustain him on the onset of any sudden hunger as the instruments which he might need. He said with an air of a man who hadn't slept too well as he lit one of his scented cigarettes, 'It's not one of my better mornings, old son, so don't give me anything too bloody-mindedly difficult.'

'A man and a woman,' Rogers said, leading him towards the abandoned car, knowing that to be brief and explicit was the thing most necessary with an early-morning and possibly edgy Twite. 'Both in the boot of that car, but I'm sure killed somewhere other than here, and somewhere not for the moment known to us. The man appears to have been shot; the woman bludgeoned. Both are in a condition suggesting they were about to get together sexually, or had already done so.' He shrugged his unknowingness.

'And your immediate problem for which you dragged me out of bed? An off-the-cuff guess at the times of their deaths?' With Rogers at his side, Twite had halted at the open boot and dropped his bag to the ground.

'Just confirmation that they are dead, of how and when they died,' Rogers said, preparing himself to re-examine visually the bodies in the now full and brilliant daylight.

'You've photographed them and I can move them?'

'Photographed and fingerprinted, Wilfred, and they're all yours.' He fished out his pipe, filled it and then scratched a match at it, preparing now to be stoical about the coming examination.

Standing behind Twite, who was now doing his own looking and would want nothing from him but silence, Rogers could appreciate how horribly pitiless death had come to the two lovers. The man Fowler appeared to be about thirty years of age with a dark moustached handsomeness, an athletic physique and, from what he could see of his exposed flesh, the tan of an open-air man. Though now with little of his mouth and chin left, he still looked to be the sort of man who would be attractive to women. Whatever he was otherwise, Rogers thought he could never have deserved this terrible ending.

There were fewer certainties about Harriet Stoner, for whose monstrously battered death he felt the greater pity. Her misshapen features no longer possessed the attractiveness she must have had to share a mutual lust with Fowler, for the skin not bloodied showed her to be a young and healthily fleshed woman in, he thought, her twenties.

He disapproved – though he knew he could be being over-critical of it – of the too-lavish verdigris green eye shadow above the yellowish-brown unseeing eyes and the over-lipsticked mouth now bloodily gaping like a scarlet tulip in what could have been the horror of her coming death. Her light brown, almost beige, hair had been worn in the contrived disorder of a later generation than his own which he couldn't find it in himself to like. What he could see of her body brought to his mind the word abundant, for everything about it seemingly was.

While Rogers was irritably pondering on why the Somebody who so manifestly Ordered Things Immaterial and Material had overlooked the simple expedient of punishing murderers with, say, an immediate and fatal bolt of lightning and by that oversight had shortened the lives of detective superintendents with their worrying about Who Had Done It, Twite was doing his visual and tactile examination of the bodies. Prodding and pressing at the dead flesh with the tips of his ungloved fingers, flexing lifeless arms and legs, sliding his hand beneath bloodied clothing and feeling the cooling skin with the back of it; opening fully eyelids already stiffening with the onset of rigor mortis and peering into the depths of the eyes for whatever information he sought in them, until finally he lowered his nose in close proximity to the dead woman's mouth and sniffed as though tasting with it the bouquet of a wine to be drunk.

Having been uncharacteristically mute during the examination, in which he had liberally dropped ash from the cigarette he held burning in his mouth, Twite straightened himself – Rogers could convince himself so easily that he could hear the creaking of a male corset as he did so – and lit a fresh cigarette from the stub of the old, following it with some red-faced coughing.

'I can certainly certify that they are dead and beyond resuscitation, dear boy,' he said, giving Rogers his medical confirmation of death, a legality the Coroner would require being given in evidence. 'The male by shooting with a sporting gun; the female by a physical trauma inflicted I'm virtually certain by the butt of the same weapon.' He pursed his mouth. 'Consider that the head was resting on a hard or firm surface when the blows – they must have been repeated savage blows – were inflicted.'

He smiled below the incongruity of his Mexican moustache. 'This diagnosis and opinion are subject to later confirmation of course. In the meantime my examination suggests that the man was shot from a very close range. Almost skin contact, I'd say, and with a shotgun cartridge. As you may see with your own constabulary issue eyes, the entry hole of the pellets is just above and behind the right ear and is more oval than circular . . .'

'I've seen it and come to the same conclusion,' Rogers intervened, not wishing even Twite to minimize his ability to read the signs of violence.

'So you have, old son, and no doubt seen that there's very little dispersion of the shot, that there's powder burn staining around the hole indicating that the gun was fired at a slight angle to the plane of the skull. It explains the torn flesh and fragmented bone in the area of the mouth and the loss of part of the jaw and the few teeth.'

'Providing we ever find the site of the killing, I'd expect to find there the bits and pieces you're missing. I'm banking on its happening hereabouts – we don't travel too far afield for what these two were seeking, do we? – so perhaps sooner than I'm prepared to guess.'

Twite grunted. He could afford to, for that wasn't his problem. 'I agree – how could I not? – that he and the poor woman seem to have readied themselves for a no doubt adulterous session and possibly died during or after it.'

Rogers, recharging his still-hot pipe, still with a sense of guilt and with the self-exaggerated prospect of charring his tongue, said, 'Will you check for it? It might be useful to know which.'

'If she allowed uncovered entry I can. Is it all that important?'

'I don't know. Probably only to a lawyer wanting to spread unhelpful confusion,' Rogers said sourly. 'In any event, they appear to have been surprised *in flagrante delicto*, and that could have occurred anywhere but in the car's boot. Or, indeed, anywhere else but inside the car which belongs to Fowler and has been checked out.' He grinned at the pathologist. 'I'm sure you were about to tell me how long they've been dead?'

'Stop pushing me, George. Not as early in the day as this. I'd say, necessarily at a guess, that they've been dead for between six and eight hours. Don't hold me to that until I've had them on my table.' He sniffed at the warming air. 'With this air temperature, not too definitely even then.'

Rogers checked the time on his wrist-watch. 'Very roughly then, between nine and eleven o'clock last night?' He saw Inspector Hassell at the encircling police cordoning tapes talking to a thickset man he assumed to be Stoner, and he signalled for them to wait until he was finished.

'It's about the time for an illicit love, I imagine,' Twite said as if it were a repugnance to him. 'Also, I'd say she'd been drinking gin not too long before she died.'

'That might be useful. I'll have the local pubs checked.' He regarded Twite thoughtfully. 'Are we at one about what must be obvious in the shooting of Fowler and the bludgeoning of Mrs Stoner? I mean, why weren't they both shot sort of thing?

Shotguns usually come double-barrelled and both would be fired in any hot-blooded killing such as this. So, a single-barrelled gun?'

'It's your guess, old son,' Twite said cautiously, 'and I'm rather on your side. Were I minded to do in a couple copulating against my interest when I had only a single-barrelled gun, then it'd certainly make sense to shoot the man first, following that up with an ungentlemanly hammering of the lady with the butt. That seems to me to be a logical sequence of events.'

Rogers jerked his head at Hassell and the thickset man. 'If you've finished for now, someone wants to see me. I'll have these two delivered at the mortuary straight away.'

'No hurry,' Twite assured him. 'I shan't be doing them until after lunch; which is . . .' – he probably lied – '. . . a working lunch and not to be interfered with by you and a brace of corpses which aren't in too much of a hurry for it anyway.'

Rogers felt that he might have something to work on in any case, though not all that much without perhaps a vengeful husband, a deserted wife or even a jealous or discarded lover to complete the sordidness and the predictability of a simple sleeping around. Whichever it was, it would be nothing to inspire higher feelings in him.


The man who had been waiting with the departed Inspector Hassell was not immediately to Rogers's liking. Manifestly a throwback to Cro-Magnon man or *Homo erectus* – it didn't worry Rogers which it was – he inspired instant dislike. Rogers thought that Stoner must feel the same about him, for when the detective said an amiable 'Good morning' to him, he growled aggressively, 'What's all this then? They're sayin' my Harriet's been killed. Is that her you've been looking at?'

He had obviously hurriedly dressed his bulky frame, which seemed not to have any neck, in a pair of light tan trousers, possibly part of a uniform, a gaudily checked jacket over a grubby white vest with trainer shoes on sockless feet. His features seemed ill suited to smiling or expressing friendliness to questioning policemen. He sported a sparse and gingerish naval beard and moustache, the former failing to conceal the prognathous jaws. His eyes were slate grey and small with the flesh beneath them sagging in thick half-moons, the left cheek badly corrugated with shiny scar tissue. Presumably just hauled out of bed, he had the puffy bloodless look of a man who had been ill for some time.

Rogers was trying hard not to believe he already had the multiple killer before him. 'I'm sorry, Mr Stoner,' he said with an appropriate gravity, 'but I did want you here to identify Mrs Stoner. I understand she lives with you and that you are the person who should identify her.'

'She said she was with a man.' Stoner appeared not to be too anxious about identifying his sister-in-law.

'Mrs Wing? She told you?'

'She's my boss, ain't she? Is it her? Harriet, I mean.'

'It is. I'm sorry about this, but she's badly hit about. You can do it?'

Stoner was impatient. 'You're sayin' I've got to, so I will,' he growled.

He stooped under the yellow tape, following Rogers to the car, standing there while the detective lifted the lid, releasing an intrusive buzzing of flies. At first it could be thought that Stoner was unable to identify the dead woman, his brutish face giving nothing away. Then he nodded his head briefly, saying unemotionally, 'That's her all right.' Looking at the dead man, his lips tightening, he turned his back on the revealed mutilations.

'I'm sorry,' Rogers sympathized with him. 'Do you recognize the man?'

'He's Fowler, Henry Fowler, an' he works here in the park. How were they killed?'

'I thought you'd be able to see that for yourself. Your sister-in-law's been battered to death; Mr Fowler shot.'

Stoner was silent for long moments, seemingly concerned with slow and weighty thought. Then he said, 'I know. I think I do. About him anyway. What time was it? When I was on duty?'

Rogers frowned. 'I imagine so. How came you to know?'

Stoner was chewing at his lip and scowling, his thick hairy fingers pulling at the material of his jacket. 'I reckon I heard it when I was doin' my rounds just before eleven last night. I took it for one of the bastards poachin' Mr Wimbush's pheasants up in Knoll Wood. I was talkin' to Mr Latouche who'd just come in an' he'd heard it too. When I got back to the office which was straight away I rang up your lot at Thurnholme which we have to do. That was a waste of time, for you wasn't about to do anything because I suppose you'd heard it too often from us and hadn't nobody to send up anyway.' He then added boorishly, 'I wrote it in the Report Book if you want to check on it.'

'I shouldn't think poaching pheasants is of much interest to the Thurnholme Police, Mr Stoner. Not these days. Poaching's a fairly regular occurrence, isn't it?'

Stoner screwed a thinking expression into his face. 'It happens an' Mr Wimbush wants it reported to the police when it does.'

'Was that the only gunshot you heard during the night?'

'I'd have reported it, wouldn't I, if it wasn't.'

'And the Mr Latouche you were talking to is the veterinary, I assume?'

'He has a night out often and we know it, but we still have to check on anybody moving around after dark.' He spat to one side of his shoes. 'Every bugger's checked on in this place because of the animals,' he added nastily. 'Including us.'

'I don't suppose you'd have a job here if that weren't the case,' Rogers said more sharply than he had intended, not liking this Cro-Magnon type any more for living up to his expectations, being a man he thought capable and willing enough to tear off one's arms. 'Mrs Stoner presumably didn't return home last night. Wouldn't you have known that?'

'Don't be bloody wet, mate,' Stoner grunted. 'I was on duty in the park from six to two last night an' when I finish I go straight to bed. What she does ain't none of my business.'

'About Mr Fowler. Did you know that he and Mrs Stoner were associating, so to speak?'

29

'I knew she was knocking about with him.' It was reasonably clear that the dead man was no friend of his.

'You don't sound as if you approved.'

'Nor I didn't,' he said, bristling.

'I imagine there's a reason, Mr Stoner,' Rogers suggested encouragingly, thinking of three or four of them. 'I'm sure you'll pass it on to me.'

If ever a man struggled with nasty subterranean frettings it was Stoner. Finally, he said, 'My brother. She's married to my brother an' I had to look after her. He'll murder me,' he added, clearly affected by the thought.

'Look after her?' Rogers echoed. 'You've just told me that what she does was none of your business.'

'You ain't hearing me right an' it didn't mean that.' There was definite hostility in him now.

'All right, but you are saying that you had to look after her. Why doesn't he look after her himself?'

'Because he can't.' Under the rising sun, sweat was now shining on his forehead. 'Because he's away and bein' his brother he asked me to.'

'I'd better have his address. I shall have to break the news of her death to him.'

Stoner shook his bullet head in refusal. 'That's my business and his. It certainly ain't yours.'

Rogers stared at him curiously. 'It's very much my business when it comes to somebody being murdered and . . .'

'Your business don't worry me, mate,' Stoner interrupted aggressively, apparently on the boil about his brother. 'I've told you what I know an' I want to think about things before I answer any more soddin' questions about what's got nothin' to do with you. You'd better do what you're paid to do about Harriet, tha's all.'

He hawked in his throat and spat, this time not far from the detective's shoes though not near enough for him to make an issue of it. Then he turned and strode away on thick legs, his shoulders hunched, his jowls flushed with his anger.

Rogers watched him go with irritated amusement, wondering what the hell had got under this ignorant bastard's thick skin and certainly now having been given a reason or two to find out what it was. He was far from being Rogers's idea of what a security guard should be, though manifestly he was somebody's. Not, he hoped, Lesley Wing's.

Stoner with his inner smouldering fitted in so beautifully as a murderous villain that the detective was already, against his better judgement, sizing him up as a suspect with a fistful of pertinent questions needing to be answered.

5

Before leaving to see Lesley Wing – something in his chest had given a slight lurch at the thought of it – Rogers had caught up with Lingard returning to the murder scene. In the absence of any significant information from him – which, given the short time the investigation had been under way, needed no excusing – Rogers had asked him to return to Headquarters and to clear his, Rogers's, desk of any correspondence, papers or files needing attention. After bringing the Assistant Chief Constable up to date and diplomatically declining on Rogers's behalf any unmeant and unwelcome offer of assistance, he was to tear off to Crouch Aughton and dig out what information he could about Laurence Stoner and his dead wife. He was then to bottle up whatever commendable impatience he had to be about and doing until Rogers decided he had further need of his assistance. He had, not for the first or second or third time, told Lingard that such had been the unalterable fate of seconds-in-command down through the years.

Rogers had organized a hard-on-the-knees ground search by twenty uniformed PCs for whatever misbegotten fragments of matter fleeing murderers might be thought to discard at the scene – they rarely did – mainly to justify to his Chief Constable, his Deputy and Assistant Chiefs, the press and the public, that every possible – even though useless – step was being taken.

Four of his DCs had been detailed to scour the landscape immediately outside the park's perimeter for householders who might have seen or heard anything significant to the enquiry when they might properly and sensibly have been indoors or in bed and asleep.

He had already initiated the closing of the entrance gates and the placing of a manned barrier beyond the bend in the road leading from the park. This, because he held that the handling and removal of the victims of a bloody murder were never a Grand Guignol for the satisfaction of the morbidly curious.

Approaching the barrier of yellow tape and its attendant uniformed PC he braked his car to a halt, seeing beyond it a man climbing from a parked brilliantly scarlet roadster coupé, obviously recently valeted, and waving at him.

Nearing Rogers's car he was seen to be a youngish forty years or more with a touch of grey in the cream hair showing from under his panama hat. Excessively slender in an elegant off-white summer suit, he wore with it a sand-coloured shirt and a banana yellow tie with a matching silk handkerchief flowering from his breast pocket. The detective thought there was a non-British look about him. He had the sunken cheeks of an ascetic and sad dark brown eyes which might be expressing a deep unhappiness and gravity as he pushed past the PC and approached.

Not giving Rogers the opportunity of getting out of his car – a rather conventional blue Vauxhall automatic that needed cleaning – he reached through the open window for him to shake his sinewy hand. 'Latouche. Jacques Pons Latouche, the veterinary surgeon,' he introduced himself, Rogers hearing in his voice not a Gallic accent, but very much what he thought to be a contrived public school accent. 'I've just heard the dreadful news. Can I be of any help?'

'Rogers, Detective Superintendent,' he answered, a little unnecessarily for the PC would have identified him to Latouche. 'I'd be grateful if you can. I was hoping to see you early. Could you lead the way to your office or surgery where we can talk?'

'Yes, pardon me,' he replied as if he had committed a *faux pas*. 'I should have waited. It isn't far.'

Climbing back in his car – the closing of its door gave out an expensive thunking sound – he did a neat three-point turn in the narrow road and accelerated away, but not before giving Rogers the opportunity of reading 'Scorpione GTi' on its tail.

Rogers hadn't visited the wildlife park before – its animals and birds apparently behaving in a more civilized manner than *Homo sapiens* – and once he was down the gradient of the service road and on to the approach road used by visitors he was able to keep the now slow-moving Latouche in view and also to take in some of the wildlife adjacent to the road.

The park appeared to have more than its fair share of the local acreage and was well wooded with heavily foliaged trees. Narrow pedestrian walks twisted through fenced-off and generously proportioned enclosures, each containing the occupants' sleeping quarters. Passing by a ditched and wired compound he saw a small herd of zebras sharing it with three huge brown-grey boulders which, closer to, he recognized as sleeping rhinoceroses. On his other side, a flock of arrogant high-stepping ostriches kept distant company with a small number of nervously alert tan and white gazelles. A pride of lions, mostly young females under the watchful eyes of two heavily maned protectors, lay resting in the shade in a tree'd football pitch-sized enclosure of long grass behind a twelve-foot high fence; definitely not high enough for the detective's peace of mind. In a similarly spacious enclosure, a small pack of shaggy grey wolves – beautiful with slanting wicked eyes – prowled nose down among thick-trunked trees while, past them, and partially visible among trees, were the grey bulks of elephants.

In passing a small lake with a complicated rock and concrete structure of chutes and diving platforms inundating itself and a small colony of black and white penguins from a gushing fountain of water that glittered iridescent in the sun, he saw coming into view the tops of purplish-brown stone-battlemented walls against a forested hillside. While impressed with what he had seen, he had had no feeling that he might be experiencing the viewing of an African veldt or a fragment of an Antarctic frozen waste, though realizing that here he was working in an environment of which he knew practically nothing.

Latouche's car was slowing down as he entered opened iron gates leading to a paved hard standing. Signposted *Private Parking*, it was adjacent to a wooden-planked drawbridge over a moat occupied by exotic ducks and geese, manifestly being the entrance to the castle. Turning in to park between Latouche's coupé and two black Prowler buggies, Rogers climbed from his car and, wholly impressed, looked up at the castle's incredibly massive structure of discoloured purple and mahogany-red stone blotched with algae. The squat and unlovely battlemented walls were set with mullioned windows, the watch towers with their constricted arrow slits looking defensively hostile in their stony austerity. Infused with the sunlight, its heat was reflected back in burning waves. It was impressive, but architecturally unpleasant, and stood massively at the foot of a steep hill, the densely packed trees of its background forming a heavily Germanic setting for it.

'You haven't seen it before?' Latouche had joined Rogers, having put a sort of smile on his good-looking face and, this near, smelling of a scent which the detective thought might more suitably be worn by a sophisticated woman.

'I'm impressed.' Rogers smiled back at him, reacting to his friendliness and paraphrasing: 'A rose red castle half as old as time. This is where you have your office?'

'My clinic actually. Inside the castle keep and through the tunnel. How old would you think it is?'

'You're forcing me to guess. The windows look a bit overdone, but I'd say the fifteen or sixteen hundreds?' The detective's appreciation of architecture didn't go back any earlier than the Georgian period.

'You're about a century or so from it, actually,' Latouche said. 'I suppose in its way it's a fake. The front is all that's left of the original castle which has been destroyed by war and neglect. It was taken over and rebuilt in the 1830s with a

Regency-style manor house at its back for living in by a re-tired colonel of an Indian Regiment called Hubbard. Hellfire Hubbard I believe he was known as, a bloodthirsty gallant who shot and had stuffed big game when not otherwise doing his stuff for your Queen Empress. Toby Wimbush, our re-spected employer, uses what's left of the ghastly collection to illustrate his great interest in the conservation of endangered species. And, I suppose, the education of our visitors from whom we get some financial support.' He grimaced. 'Sorry about that, I hadn't intended to lecture you, but anything rather than think about poor Harriet.'

'I'm interested, and I appreciate how you must feel,' Rogers assured him. 'Do we go in?' He thought that Latouche might be on the verge of crying, and weeping men could embarrass him.

'It's not actually in the castle. That's mostly all front. It hides Mr Wimbush's private apartments in the original house and where a few of us have accommodation.' Latouche abruptly turned back to the undisguised sadness he had earlier dis-played. 'I'm sorry. You wanted to speak to me about Harriet's death and I'm desperately trying not to think of her as she now is.'

Rogers followed him over the drawbridge and through a short stone-walled tunnel – the air in it struck chill even in the growing heat of the day – with a wooden-panelled door in each side and a huge latched-back double iron gate at its end, this giving entry into a circular high-walled courtyard referred to by Latouche as the keep.

Built against the courtyard wall were modern portable single-floor office buildings and, in following Latouche to one of them, Rogers passed an ancient ten-foot long black cannon mounted on a central plinth, its ugly muzzle pointing out through the iron gate. The late Colonel Hubbard, Rogers de-cided, had not been a man to face aggressively at the business end of a gun.

Latouche's clinic, a fairly spacious low-ceilinged room, had in it his large leather-topped desk bearing up under a long row of text and reference books and a telephone; a plain metal desk on which stood an electronic typewriter; a pair of white filing cabinets, trays of papers, a second telephone and several telephone directories, some of which were obviously foreign. A small photocopier and a coffee maker shared an electric switch on a shelf near the desk. There was a faint smell of past coffee percolations mingling with Latouche's own body scent.

Rogers, invited to be seated on a metal and plastic chair at what he assumed to be Harriet Stoner's desk, waited while Latouche took up the commanding position of the huge green leather chair behind his own desk, appearing to compose himself for what he might consider an unpleasantness.

Rogers asked, 'Who told you about the deaths, Mr Latouche?'

'Lesley Wing, our chief security officer.' He looked concerned. 'That was all right, wasn't it?'

'It's no great crime,' Rogers assured him amiably. 'You know how they both died, do you?'

'No. Do I need to?'

'I think so. Mrs Stoner was battered to death . . .' – the veterinary had winced at that – '. . . and Henry Fowler was shot. I feel it necessary to also tell you that they appear to have been making, or about to make, love when they were killed.'

That had hurt Latouche and tears brimmed in his eyes. He swallowed and said, near to a whisper, 'I'm sorry. I can't seem to accept she's so terribly dead . . . that she won't be here at her desk any more. I'm fond of her, Mr Rogers . . .' He was silent while the big white-faced clock on the wall ticked away the passing seconds and he rubbed the back of his hand over his eyes. 'Could I see her before she's taken away? I'd like to say goodbye to her.'

Rogers spoke gently, understanding the man's distress. 'She's already being taken to the mortuary in Abbotsburn. In any case I don't think it's advisable. Beating a woman to death doesn't . . . well, it's not a pretty operation.'

When Latouche made no answer, he asked, 'How long had she been with you?'

'Eighteen months or so. We got on so well together. On a working together basis, of course,' he added quickly.

And as lovers? Rogers wanted to ask, for it wouldn't be at all surprising had they been. Instead, he said, 'She was living in the village with Stoner, her brother-in-law, I understand. Is that so?'

A shadow crossed the veterinarian's face. 'May I be frank about this?'

'I'd be grateful,' Rogers assured him, though not so grateful that he was about to believe every word offered him. His eyes, had Latouche seen into them, would have probably showed his cynicism over such promises of frankness.

'Harriet is – I should say was – married to Will Stoner's brother who, I believe, is a thoroughgoing bad hat and in what Harriet called trouble somewhere, though what or where she never said. This brother apparently asked or pressed Will Stoner to look after her until he was relieved of the trouble he was in.'

'Was his trouble concerned with the police wherever it is he lives?' It was hot in the office and Rogers's trousers were sticking to the PVC covering on the chair on which he uncomfortably sat.

Latouche appeared to be metaphorically wringing his hands. 'I don't honestly know. Harriet would never tell me. Nor did I really wish to know.'

'What did she call him? His given name?'

'Ah.' He put a small-knuckled fist to his chin and frowned in thought. 'I'm almost sure she called him Larry. Mostly, of course, she said "my husband".'

Latouche had acted a little theatrically there and Rogers filed it away for his future reference. He said, 'So she lived with Will Stoner as a sort of lodger. Has he a wife? Any family with him?'

'He had a wife, but she died before Harriet arrived.' Latouche shook his head in negation, flopping a thick strand of cream-coloured hair over his forehead. 'I know what you're thinking, but I'm sure not. I thought the same when she first arrived and Stoner got permission to have her as his guest or lodger. She and he had to see Toby Wimbush to get his authority, so it had to be right. I was, thank God, mistaken in

37

what I thought. She genuinely disliked him, and if you'd met him you'd know why. Between the two of us he's a most objectionable and surly brute of a man and, anyway, not to my knowledge particularly interested in women as such.'

Each time he had finished answering Rogers in an apparent resurgence of normality he would sink back to an expression of his earlier grief and sadness. Rogers had to accept that he had had a genuine affection for his lost secretary.

'While I'm conscious of your feelings for Harriet,' he said, 'I think it right to say that she hadn't the same lack of interest in other men, had she? She was with Henry Fowler when they died and, as I've already said, the circumstances of their dying do confirm that they were lovers.' He kept his gaze fixed on the unhappy man who looked wounded by his words and whose fingers were agitatedly restless on the blotting-pad in front of him.

'And I feel that you need an answer to that,' Latouche said almost inaudibly.

'If not from you, then from someone else. You did say you wished to be frank with me; please be so.' Rogers had given him the full force of his penetrating, rather forbidding stare. A card notice on the veterinarian's desk reading *Thank you for not smoking* wasn't adding to the sum of his own equanimity.

'Well,' Latouche said, not too willingly, 'we are rather stuck here away from Thurnholme Bay or from anywhere else that's fun. Harriet was a lovely girl, though not quite one of us, of course, and I imagine needing a man's friendship, even more so in what appeared to me to be an unhappy and unsatisfactory marriage. She went out for evening meals and so on with several of the staff, though it wouldn't be right for me to guess who they were. I certainly didn't know she was involved as seriously as you say with Henry Fowler, though I'm not surprised for he was a nice chap and a good match for her.'

'A question of her general morality, Mr Latouche,' Rogers said carefully, and guessing rather wildly. 'Would you think that her relationships with men approached promiscuity? A generosity with the use of her body, or her use of theirs?'

Latouche had clearly winced at this. 'She was a very friendly and happy girl. How far her friendliness extended to the men she went out with was her business and none of mine. I wouldn't know and it isn't for me to guess that either.' That was rebuke for Rogers's line of questioning and he leaned back in his chair, chewing at his lower lip as if in a sadly thoughtful mood. Then, he added in the ensuing silence he seemed obliged to fill, 'I'm sorry, but it doesn't appear that I can help you much.'

Rogers said, more sternly than he had intended, 'I don't actually think that's so, Mr Latouche. While it may not be right for you to do any guessing, none of it does very much for the woman you employed and of whom you say you were fond. In fact I have no need of guesses, but for you to tell me what I believe you to know.' His gaze was steady on the veterinarian, forcing him to listen and understand. 'I would have thought that you owed Mrs Stoner a moral duty to give me the information I've asked you for. If you have any knowledge of any person with whom she has been recently associating, I want you to name him – or them. You are not accusing anybody of anything if that's your worry; that's for me to do if I later have evidence to do so.' He left the words hanging in the air, underlining them with his hard discomfiting stare and willing him to open up.

When Latouche did, it was with an almost angry reluctance. 'If I am forced to name names,' he said stiffly, 'it's on the understanding that they were mentioned by Harriet in casual conversation to me as men she had gone out with and nothing more. One was Harris Bloor, one of the security guards; the other was Quentin Coope, and he's a young trainee keeper.' With that, he shut tight his lips, signifying clearly that that was all.

'And they're both still here?' Rogers asked.

Latouche nodded, then said, 'There's nothing more, I hope?'

'Just a minor something or two and nothing to do with what you've just said.' Rogers made his voice sound accommodating. What he most wanted to ask – for he believed it to be so – was a probably brutal 'Had you yourself enjoyed Harriet's sexual favours?' but decided not yet. Instead, he asked, 'Do you know where she came from? Her previous address sort of thing?'

'Not, I'm afraid. At least, not to hand, but I recall somewhere in Crouch Aughton.' He looked as if thinking hard, then said apologetically, 'I probably have it somewhere in the office if I can think where to look.' He brightened a little. 'I do recall her name before she was married, if that helps. It was Gager and I remember it because I've a cousin of that name.'

'And your impression is that she didn't much care for her husband?'

'I'm sure she didn't.'

'Or the brother she lived with?'

'Of that, I'm certain.'

'Do you recall being checked by him last night?'

Latouche frowned. 'I don't know that I agree I was checked. I certainly met him while he was on his rounds and I was returning here to my rooms. Common courtesy suggested I should speak to him. How do you know that?' he demanded with spirit.

'It was mentioned to me,' Rogers prevaricated. 'I understand you were with him when you heard a gunshot. Were you able to locate the sound?'

'Yes, I was. Stoner said it sounded as if it came from Knoll Wood; something about poachers after Toby Wimbush's pheasants that he's trying to naturalize, and he'd heard the same thing before. It sounded to me as if it did.'

'Where were you both when you heard this?'

'Near the restaurant, at the public entrance.' He stared hard at the detective, some of his apparently natural authority showing. 'Why are you so interested in that?'

'It could have been that you heard the shot that killed Fowler.'

'Holy Joseph!' The veterinarian was horrified. 'I hadn't connected the two.'

'Apparently Stoner did. Later this morning, of course. What time was it when you heard the shot?'

'Oh, God!' He beat his forehead with the heel of his hand. 'That's when she died, wasn't it? It must have been about eleven. Or just after. I can't honestly be certain.'

'Could you identify the sort of gun from which the shot might have been fired?'

'Absolutely not,' he groaned. 'And, please, don't . . .' he trailed off.

'It appears that Stoner could,' Rogers persisted.

Latouche looked drained, flapping a despairing hand. 'I don't wish to be offensive . . . refusing and all that, but my business is with the animals and birds and the reptiles, and I think for the time being I must allow my fellow men and women to take care of themselves. I'm sorry . . .'

Rising from his chair, Rogers said reasonably amiably for such a hot day and at least an hour away from his last smoke, 'I wish I could do the same, Mr Latouche, but I think that the rather difficult Police Authority who employ me would like something done about finding the psychopath who happens to be operating inside this park.'

Leaving, he thought that despite their differences he rather liked this man – was it Jacques Pons Latouche he'd remembered his name to be? – though he was not too sure about his attitude to the bloody murder of a woman he employed and for whom he obviously held affection; though, indeed, despite appearances he might be the sort of man who could wish the killer to be put down like a dangerously rabid dog. Which was something with which the detective could agree, though without making a parallel case of an unfortunate dog. It was also something which, in the absence of a Divine and immediate thunderbolt, he kept wisely hidden in the secret recesses of his own thinking.

6

Lesley Wing was waiting for Rogers at the exit end of the stone tunnel, and he again experienced the pleasurable lurching in his chest at the sight of her, dressed beautifully as she was in a summerweight skirt and epauletted jacket, obviously her uniform though there were neither badges nor insignia on it.

With her high-cheekboned elfin face and spare figure she again reminded him of the seemingly hell-bent-on-discarding-him Angharad. This went with a foreboding of future trouble with his easily diverted interest in attractive women of Lesley Wing's stamp and persuasion. It was coming near to one of the occasions when, exaggeratedly, he admitted, he would begin to wish that he had been born a neutered male.

He joined her, smiling happily. 'It's been a long time,' he said. It was his verbal test of possible compatibility.

She smiled back at him in passing it. 'I thought you'd never make it.'

She wasn't another Angharad and he didn't wish her to be, but seeing her mouth curling in the friendly smile, the warmth in her expressive brown eyes looking up at him, stirred in him, even coffeeless at ten thirty in mid-morning, a frisson of sexual desire.

'I remember now,' he said. 'I asked you to have your chap Bloor available for me.'

'He's at home, warned to leap out of bed at your need,' she told him. 'But I've something you may think is more important.'

'I'm sure it will be,' he agreed with an uncharacteristic docility. Bloor was the security guard on the shift following the thuggish Stoner; a man he had obviously to see though not with any apparent urgency. He was content to listen in the cool shade of the tunnel.

'You may not be kept too long,' she said soberly, 'but I think I know where Harriet and Henry Fowler may have been killed.'

He searched her face for guile, finding none. 'Thank God!' He was cheerfully optimistic and therefore flippant. 'I'll love you for ever if you do.'

She frowned slightly. 'Please don't put too much certainty in it. I said I only *think* I know.'

'Of course. I'm sorry, Mrs Wing.' He had been too enthusiastic. 'I won't take it as anything more. Was it in Knoll Wood?'

She jerked her head. 'Knoll Wood? No, it wasn't. Who told you that?'

'Nobody, actually.' He thought his wallowing in clumsiness had upset her and he was immediately contrite. 'At least, nothing more than what Stoner told me about his hearing a shot coming from Knoll Wood. A pheasant poacher, he thought, and he recorded it in your Report Book.'

'That's where I saw it, though I didn't connect it with the murders. He told you nothing else?'

'Only that he heard it about eleven last night. I don't even know where Knoll Wood is yet.'

'It's behind where we're going.'

'I'm sorry,' he said placatingly. 'I must be confusing you.'

'He said nothing else?' She paused as Latouche entered the tunnel, smiling vaguely and flapping his hand almost apologetically at them in passing out into the sunshine.

'No,' Rogers answered her. 'Other than, perhaps . . .' – he smiled at the recollection of it – '. . . advising me to get stuffed.'

'That's Stoner all over,' she said. 'I should have warned you he's a barbarian. I'm hoping to take you to a summerhouse belonging to the park estate, and which is situated in Hubbard's Copse.' She wrinkled her nose, probably a sign that he was out of the doghouse. 'It's pretty ancient, the date – seventeen-hundred something – has been cut out over the door, and though it's been listed as a protected building it's been allowed to start dying a natural death by decay and everybody's indifference.'

Rogers had been holding his pipe in his fist and she could have hardly failed to see it. She broke off to say in mock bossiness, 'You're making me nervous with your pipe. We're not inside anywhere so why don't you smoke it?'

While he was stuffing it with tobacco, she said, 'Some of the staff use the summerhouse during the season – such as now – for eating their sandwiches rather than using the restaurant when it's crammed with visitors.'

She was reading his face, probably trying to see from his put-on non-expression how this was going down. Seemingly

43

satisfied, she continued. 'It's supposed to be haunted by the ghost of an eighteen-year-old stableman called Richard Green who died there in 1882. His ashes were discovered there together with the ends of his fingers and his completely un-burnt feet from his ankles down, wearing untouched socks and boots which were the only things identifying him. Nothing else was burned – certainly not the summerhouse – though the chair near which his ashes were found was charred.'

'I've dealt with one of those myself,' Rogers said. 'It sounds much like a case of spontaneous human combustion. Curious that. It doesn't occur very often and when it does it goes against the grain to accept that it can happen.'

'Yes or no,' she said, seeming to be pleased that Rogers was possibly in accord with what she was saying, 'there was certainly a scandal attached to it. Lady Letitia, the elder daughter of Lord Wildbore, the then owner of the castle, simultaneously went missing, eventually being found wandering the streets of Abbotsburn in a confused and distressed condition by the local police, about which you probably know.'

'Not so, Mrs Wing,' Rogers said sardonically. 'It was a little before my time. Did she say what happened?'

'Apparently she did at the inquest where the local newspaper report failed to name her father and referred to her as a heavily veiled lady whose name was withheld because she was said to be suffering a nervous breakdown. She said in evidence that she was giving Green his instructions concerning the exercising of her hunter mare when a most peculiar expression came over his face and blue flames burst from the area of his stomach. His terrifying screaming so shocked her that, temporarily losing her reason, as the local newspaper had it, she ran in horror from the summerhouse, not recalling who or where she was until found in Abbotsburn by a Police Sergeant Bunning. It finished with the Coroner delivering his finding that Green had died as the result of a visitation by God or something similar.'

'Interesting,' Rogers said, trying hard not to look too po-faced and not needing it shouted at him to understand what she was meaning. 'I take it that this summerhouse is notorious for being used, and continuing to be used, for what we might call assignations of an improper nature?'

She cocked her head at him, almost smiling. 'That's a nice way of putting it and it's quite deplorable, isn't it? You think not a bad suggestion?'

'Worthy of one of Her Majesty's most engaging and lately retired commissioned officers,' he told her with blatant flattery. 'It being understood that the summerhouse still has the same attraction for intending lovers such as Harriet and Henry, yes?'

'It's known.' She was neither censorious nor approving. 'Its ambience appears to provoke all sorts of appetites.'

'Savagery being one of them,' he said, his voice hard in recalling the horrors in the car's boot; then, tersely, 'Bloody unforgivable savagery!'

Seeing her suddenly startled expression at his outburst, he said, 'I'm sorry, Mrs Wing. It's only that I saw those two in my mind again. You've been researching on the summerhouse, it seems?'

'Not really. It's all in a booklet Toby Wimbush had printed on the history of Caldbeck Castle. You can buy it in the souvenir shop if you're interested.'

'I'm relying on your taking me there.' He smiled.

'Of course. And before we go on with it, I'd prefer that you'd not keep calling me Mrs Wing; it sounds stuffy somehow. I use it only for my position here at the park, and the name *is* Lesley.'

With their turning into the car-parking area – Rogers saw an empty space where Latouche's coupé had been – she said, 'We'll go in one of the buggies, if you don't mind. I don't think your car would make it on the summerhouse's path.'

The seat of the buggy on to which she directed him was scalding hot and he grimaced at the pain of it, at the possible damage it might be doing to what he thought of as his undercarriage. When she slid into the driving seat with no suggestion that she had similarly suffered, the buggy's lack of width forced her into what was for him a pleasurable bodily contact.

Backing the buggy out and turning it full circle within its

45

own short length, she drove it out through the gates and into the road already busy with walking visitors. Being battery-driven, its movement was virtually noiseless if held at a strolling pace, which seemed to be its happy maximum.

He was content to sit in silence and view the animal and bird enclosures, to remain so intimately close to her body though careful to blow his smoke away from her, until they reached a turn-off leading to the opposite side of the park. This led into what he assumed was the green quietness of Hubbard's Copse where the buggy was slowed down on approaching a gate signposted *Private: No Entry*.

Lesley Wing, slowing the buggy to less than a crawl, nudged the closed gate open with the blunt front of it and drove through, the gate swinging shut behind them. It had needed a certain well-measured finesse to be able to do it and it wasn't necessary for him to do much thinking in assuming that she had driven through it before.

A short way along a worn brick path in a tunnel of green which Rogers was certain would have accommodated his own car, she pulled into a sun-baked clearing out of sight of the gate where the summerhouse stood, dappled gold and green under a huge beech tree at its perimeter. Beyond it, through the trees, he could see the slick shininess of a small stream, hearing water moving in the silence of the heavily foliaged wood.

After Rogers had taken in the exterior of what was a beautifully proportioned half-timbered octagonal building of reportedly ill repute, he dismounted from the buggy and walked slowly, almost meditatively, to it, leaving Lesley Wing remaining seated.

Refilling and lighting his pipe as he walked as if by unthinking rote, he tried to concentrate his mind away from his distracting companion. Near to, he could see that the arched windows, virtually hidden by swathes of green growth hanging from the guttering, were set in deep recesses and largely glassless. Wild plants growing below the windows had grown tall, aiding in shutting out light. The door and doorway, not too improbably, he thought, having been made from timber left over from the building of a medieval cathedral, had a carved 1789 just discernible on the lintel. Above, the roof shingles appeared to be wooden, but were now dark green with pincushion moss covering them. There was a smell of ancient years about its dying richness, and if Rogers had seen the pallidly dead face of Richard Green staring at him through one of the disintegrating windows, he would not have been too startled.

'Are you coming in?' he called to the waiting Lesley Wing, his voice sudden in the clearing, frightening off two pigeons in a clattering of wing feathers.

When she joined him, he said, 'You're in this with me, Lesley. I take it you're not worried about what we find?'

'No.' She didn't look it either. 'But I wasn't intending to interfere uninvited.'

He looked quizzically at her. 'I thought I could ask you to go on being a sort of unofficial colleague of mine. After all, I am working in what is your bailiwick and still trying to find my way about the place.'

'I'd like to, George,' she answered him, and his name had never sounded so intimate as she had said it, though he conceded there had been Angharad and a few others he couldn't immediately call to mind.

She nodded at the door. 'A big secret; it's not locked. The key's lost and it never is.'

Opening it and stepping inside on to a brick floor worn smooth from long use, he smelt the mustiness of decaying wood, the light filtering through the windows – there were seven of them – casting unhealthy-looking greenish flesh tones on them both.

The one-roomed wooden-walled interior – colonized extensively by web-spinning spiders – in which there seemed to be a muffled silence, was furnished with a smallish crimson velvet upholstered *chaise-longue* showing stains and bald patches where not covered with a blue-patterned rug thrown over the head of it – he thought it possible that this could be the actual piece of furniture on which the Lady Letitia had lost her honour, if not her virginity, in the no doubt lusty embrace of her groom – a battered escritoire with pigeon-holes, its attendant wooden chair padded with flaking leather, and a small badly scratched wooden table with ornamental legs. The furniture, apart from two anachronistic plastic café chairs, was worm-eaten and disintegrating, easily guessed at as being early Victorian and, in the cynical Rogers's judgement, probably worth more as such than the whole of his annual salary. There was no means of lighting there and nothing immediately visible to suggest that bloody murder had been committed in it; unless it was its atmosphere in which he thought he could feel a brooding unease.

Lesley Wing broke the heavy silence between them. 'Although I didn't say it, I was so sure,' she said with disappointment in her voice.

'We haven't looked yet,' he told her. He didn't wish to feel sorry for her, for that would be undeserved. 'In fact, we haven't yet started. Murderers *have* been known to clear up the mess after they've done it.'

Chewing at the stem of his gone-out pipe, believing by now that in the enervating heat he must be smelling embarrassingly like a hard-ridden horse, he walked over to the *chaise-longue* and, without touching it, stared at it, assessing it as a piece of furniture on which it might be possible to make love to a woman without occasionally falling off or even burning oneself to death by a spontaneous combustion. Moving to its rear he crouched and looked under it, grunting something that sounded like satisfaction and then standing. Stepping to the wall adjacent to its back and kneeling, cursing only just audibly the brick floor's hardness on his knees, he picked with his pocket-knife at tiny wormholes in the wood. After a minute or two he rose to his feet, his aching knees giving him hell.

'Bull's-eye, Lesley,' he said approvingly. 'We've shotgun pellets in the wall, so it seems that our two bodies died on the *chaise-longue* while making love or something.' He moved to the front of it. 'Be with me while I reveal all.' He added inaudibly under his breath, 'I hope.'

'Does this mean I was right?' she said, knowing that it did, but wanting him to say it.

'Happily, yes . . . for us, anyway.' He held the corner of the rug thrown on to the *chaise-longue* and raised it slowly, then, as tentatively, lifted the cushion exposed beneath it, both instinctively recoiling from the swarm of large flies released from their feeding on the clots of dark blood in which could be seen fragments of discoloured flesh growing tufts of hair and broken jaw teeth.

It was obviously only part of the whole, but enough, and he let the cushion and corner of the rug fall back, tucking it in to keep out the flies. 'You saw?' he asked.

She had shuddered, but remained composed. 'Enough,' she replied, then softly, 'Poor Harriet. And poor Henry, too. I hope their guardian angels are looking after them a little better than they've done so far.'

'I'm with you there,' Rogers agreed amiably, now reasonably pleased and feeling more optimistic than what he actually had could justify. 'I think you'll find that guardian angels have an overrated reputation for being always on the job.' More seriously, guiding her out into the sunlight, he said, 'There's something you can do for me, if you would.'

She held his gaze as if looking for the intent behind his words. 'I'd be glad to if that's what you want. It really is a part of my responsibility, isn't it?'

'It's a good way of looking at it, and I'd be very much obliged to you.' Shamefully, the darkish undergrowth of needs in the basement of his mind – he had always considered that it was nothing really to do with him at all – was imagining holding her in his arms on something like the *chaise-longue* he had just seen, even as his higher mind sought for what he was about to say. 'For a start, I can't now leave the summerhouse unguarded, so I'd be grateful if you'd return to where the bodies were found, pick up one of the uniformed PCs waiting around in the Murder Wagon for someone to tell him what to do and bring him back here. Then, perhaps, you'd take me back to my car.'

'It's possibly a silly suggestion,' she said hesitantly, 'but remembering the horrible death of Lady Letitia's stableman, it could be that the summerhouse holds in itself the means to provoke violent deaths – its ambience, I suppose I mean.'

Rogers grimaced. 'I'd never throw out the possibility, but even if it did, it couldn't help or influence my thinking about who killed them.'

'No, I see that. It was just a thought.'

'Before you leave and I forget, did Harriet go equipped with a handbag or somesuch? There wasn't one in the car, and there's obviously not one in here.'

'Yes,' she said, 'she did. A very nice leather shoulder bag. I don't think she'd go anywhere without it.'

As she started to move away, he said, trying hard not to be too damned pompous, 'Just one thing, Lesley. I may not be all that forthcoming from my side with information and opinion. That'll mean no more than I'm conforming, as I'm required, to the official Secrets Act.'

Watching her climb into her buggy and drive away, he leafed mentally through the provisions of both the Act and Police Regulations, to remind himself that there was nothing in either to bar him from making love to a civilian security officer should the opportunity present itself and he was in the mood not to resist so compelling a temptation. As with the majority of civilized males, he normally acted out his role as *Homo sapiens* but, beset by temptation, could easily revert to *Homo erectus* in the fullest physical sense.

Filling his pipe and lighting it while he waited, he thought morosely of his own inconstancies and of the niceness of Angharad for whom he had a deep affection, and whom he was soon likely to lose to a hugely advantaged circuit judge with his own yacht and an attachment to a chambers ready to take Angharad into its legal maw.

7

Rogers, dropped at the castle gate by Lesley and promised that Security Guard Harris Bloor – he was tall, bearded and strikingly good-looking, she had said – would be in the parade room in double-quick time and then at the detective's convenience, sat in his car with both front doors open, unwilling to be parboiled in the use of the force radio.

Smoking his pipe free from possible censorious eyes, he did some hard thinking. He was far from happy that he knew much of use about the dead Harriet Stoner and her loutish brother-in-law, and not too ecstatic about the dead Fowler either. They seemed at the moment to be lacking in substance; characters with no comprehensible background and hovering in his consciousness like dark clouds. Nor, in his thinking, had he overlooked the possibility that in the night's darkness – there had been no moon – Fowler may have been killed in error for somebody else.

The words 'foregone conclusions' rarely entered his mind, being in his opinion a block on analytical thinking; yet now the remembered smell and taste of Stoner's unpleasantness was doing just that, blinding him to as yet unknown and unmet possibilities. Were he asked to classify the murders, he might, just to shut someone up and to dampen down unwanted speculation, say that they appeared to be the almost acceptable *crime passionnel* as the French gendarmerie might have it when they didn't know exactly what.

Contacting the elegant Lingard on the radio – he sounded somewhat miffed at having to deal with Rogers's paperwork – he gave him a run-down on the now known scene of the double murder and on the little he knew of Harriet née Gager, William Stoner with a Royal Marines background – he described the brutish guard pithily, but colourfully – and Laurence Stoner of no background at all but with a murky reputation. He then told him to change tack and to go to Crouch Aughton as a matter of urgency and to return to brief him with every detail short of a run-down on the family's genealogical chart; particularly to obtain answers to why the security guard Stoner was seeking to discourage him, Rogers, from having his brother told of his wife's death, and why she was living with her brother-in-law anyway.

When Lingard had acknowledged that and said it was already in the bag, Rogers told him to grab Sergeant Magnus –

who was to drop everything he had been doing – and order him back to Castle Caldbeck immediately where he was to find his way to the summerhouse in Hubbard's Copse and metaphorically to take it apart in his search for evidence pointing to whoever had so brutally murdered the two lovers.

He was about to close down when he remembered one other floating matter. He said, 'Not finished yet, David. When you're back from Crouch Aughton, find time to trawl through Mrs Stoner's room. I don't know what you're to look for, but whatever it is might prove useful. And while I'm with you, it might be good policy if you'd contact Mrs Wing and take her with you. I'll mention it to her when I see her.'

With all that off his chest he relit his pipe and leaned back to wait for the approach of a bearded man with the look of a Bachelor of Arts.

When he came, a six-footer in tan twills with brown grey-speckled hair and a small beard and moustache, striding the road with a purposeful air, he entered the passage without having once glanced in the detective's direction, yet, to Rogers, clearly aware of his presence.

Following him, Rogers saw him enter the door of one of the offices marked *SECURITY*, leaving it ajar. Bloor was standing in the room waiting for him. He was eye to eye with Rogers in height; his small dense beard and thin moustache were Tudor Elizabethan, his face narrow and seemingly set in an expression of polite arrogance. He had an athlete's muscled neck, bottle-neck shoulders and a flat belly, yet withal looking donnish. He appeared anything but a security guard and the detective thought that given the necessary heterosexuality he must be an attractive number for any properly constituted woman.

When he spoke in answer to Rogers's introduction of himself and the production of his warrant card, it was in an expected-to-be-listened-to confident voice. 'Mrs Wing asked me to meet you here,' he said. 'She's told me more about the deaths of Harriet and Henry and asked me to give you what help I can.' He gestured with his hand at a wooden chair behind a small sloping desk with a document-concealing ornamented fillet. 'Please take a seat. I'll sit on one of the visitors' chairs.'

What Lesley had called the parade room seemed to be exactly that, for he had seen many police parade rooms in his service. It probably doubled also as the guardroom as she had originally called it. Apart from the desk at which he sat, there were three wooden chairs, four tall clothing and equipment lockers, a metal stand with a radio transmitter on it, a narrow cupboard and a second door with a *Chief Security Officer* board – obviously Lesley's – on it. The room smelled of cleaning mousse and wax polish, irritatingly free of tobacco smoke.

'I'm assuming you knew Mrs Stoner and Fowler as fellow employees at the park and therefore fairly well?' Rogers said.

Bloor nodded, a little cursorily.

'When you arrived at the scene this morning, were you able to see the bodies?'

He shook his head. 'No, and I didn't wish to. I didn't even know who they were until afterwards.'

'All right. I'll leave them for the moment and go back to last night. You were on the two to ten late-night shift, finishing this morning following on after Mr Stoner who booked off at two o'clock?'

Bloor nodded again, and Rogers hoped he wasn't to be a man niggardly of words. He liked garrulous, almost unstoppable interviewees.

'Did he say anything to you before booking off?'

'He said there wasn't anything much to report, other than he thought he'd heard a car driving away from the main entrance gate, and that a poacher seemed to be briefly active in the upper part of Knoll Wood.' Before answering, Bloor had manifestly chewed over its relevance in his mind.

'Did he mention times?'

'Only about the car which he said he'd heard about eleven thirty. That wasn't important because the entrance gates abut on to the public road and it's not unusual for cars to be pulled into the lay-by near them. After he'd gone, I saw he'd entered that in the Report Book and also that he'd heard the poacher's gun being fired at eleven. The usual inconsequential stuff,' he added a little disparagingly, 'though I must say I haven't heard poachers on the job for over three months.'

Rogers had the impression that whatever Stoner did or did not do, it wouldn't meet with Bloor's approval. 'Did you yourself see or hear anything unusual last night? Apart, of course, from your coming on the scene this morning?'

'No. It was promising to be one of those uneventful boring nights. Nobody we knew or didn't know moving about until daylight; no noises other than those made by the animals and some of the birds.'

'Would you not have heard the car carrying the bodies approaching the service gates at four this morning?'

'Almost certainly not. We operate on prearranged patrols and at four on this particular night I would be on the opposite side of the park, on Point A.' He paused, searching Rogers's face. 'Stoner would have told you about Quentin Coope, would he?'

'You might be surprised to hear that he and I don't hit it off too well, and he's told me very little about anything.'

Bloor smiled white-toothed and it transformed his face. 'A churlish and aggressive bastard, isn't he? He is in everyone's book. I mention Coope because he's usually about the park at all hours of the night and might be a source of information for you.'

'And he's who? And what?'

'He's a gap year student waiting to go up to university and using his otherwise unemployed months working here as a trainee keeper.' Bloor was gently amused, scratching a finger at his beard. 'He's about all hours of the night – God knows how he finds the stamina for it – because he's a budding entomologist, specializing in the *Noctuidae*: night-flying moths, as you probably know.'

'Yes,' Rogers said, having only heard something of them in the far past, but not about to admit it.

'You'd know also that the moths are much attracted to mercury-vapour lighting which we happen to use in vulnerable areas of the park. Coope goes round these and his other moth traps at intervals – only he knows the times, but mainly between ten and one o'clock this month of the year – carrying a light aluminium ladder and his jars. And a net too, naturally. He might – only just might – be of help to you. I say

54

'only just might" because he operates on a single-minded system of his own, oriented on moths and on moths alone.'

Bloor had hunched forward with his elbows on his knees, his bearded chin cupped in his hands. If it was a sort of body language, the detective didn't know what it meant.

'I'm grateful,' he said. 'How old is he? And do you know where he comes from?'

'He's eighteen or thereabouts I imagine, and I guess from Lancashire. He speaks occasionally of Southport.'

'And where does he live locally?'

'With Harry Halcro and his wife in the village.' He could see a not-knowingness in Rogers's expression and he added, 'Mr Halcro's the head keeper, and a fine chap he is too. He'll give you every help he can.'

'I'll see them both.' He smiled. 'While I'm about it, are you in the village as well?'

'Yes, though my status being that of unaccompanied divorcee I'm reduced to occupying a room at the God Bless the British Army inn.'

'Could we get back to Stoner? Am I right in understanding that there's little liking between him and you, and possibly the others in the park?'

'Ah!' Bloor growled. 'I think you may be right there.' He lifted his elbows from his thighs, sitting more upright. 'Somebody's been talking, I imagine. You mean specifically about his landing one on me over l'*affaire* Harriet?'

'Specifically, yes,' Rogers agreed as if he already knew. 'I'd like to know the rights and wrongs of it.'

Bloor smoothed his beard between forefinger and thumb. 'It was a couple of months back and wasn't actually that much of a brawl.' He grinned with an unexpected boyishness. 'And what do you know. Even for a dedicated advocate of peace at nearly any price, it was worth it. He'd apparently found out about Harriet and me – which was already dying the death, by the way – and he landed one on me here in the parade room in the middle of telling me off. In the process of defending myself I kicked him in his shins and while he was worrying about that chopped him in his throat, smack on his gullet.' He pulled a face as if wincing in severe pain. 'It made the stupid bugger fall down on his face and puke up his supper or whatever it was. Then he had to clean it up before Mrs Wing made one of her visits. It was worth it. For me, at any rate. We now manage to speak to each other on the job, but that's about all.'

'About par for the course and I don't blame you.' Rogers was now about to make it a man-to-man discussion about his affair with Mrs Stoner. 'However,' he said, 'professionalism apart, I'm soft-centred on women who have been murdered and I'm particularly unsettled about how your Harriet died so brutally.' Staring unblinkingly at Bloor he could detect no particular emotion surfacing in his expression. 'You were fond of her, naturally?'

'I liked her well enough, though you have to weigh that against the only alternatives here as being someone's unsatisfied wife – just not done, old chap – or one of the big cats. I'm joking, of course,' he added, showing white teeth again, 'but you know what I mean.'

He shrugged. 'Who really knows anything about women anyway? She was an easygoing girl with an educated intelligence; too nice a girl to need to spread it around the *hoi polloi*, which she seemed to be doing, though I've no real proof of that. After I'd been thumped, it so happened that I didn't have the need to go back to her as I might have done and possibly risk having my head kicked in by a resurrected Stoner.'

'You've ideas of who constituted the *hoi polloi* you mention?'

'Of course I have.' He shook his head. 'None, however, whom you might reasonably believe to be associated with the killings, so I'm afraid that's for you to find out. My instinct tells me never to say too many hard words about somebody else's morality or lack of it. You'll forgive me, I hope?'

'I can't tear out your fingernails about it,' Rogers said, amiably enough. 'A delicate question. Could I ask where you and Harriet met for your social intercourse? Your room? Her room? Or, say, the summerhouse?' He waited while Bloor thought about it.

'You're a nosy bugger, aren't you?' Bloor said, his expression sardonic. 'All right, it's your job and I don't really mind. It was her room when we were sure that Stoner was definitely somewhere else. Otherwise . . .' – he shrugged – '. . . it was the summerhouse, though that could be dangerous with no rear door for an honourable retreat.'

'It puzzles me why Stoner should object so violently to you or indeed anyone else he thought could be making love to Harriet. She's his sister-in-law, not his wife and I can't imagine his being over moralistic about it.'

'His own wife died about three years ago, but it could be family honour and all that stuff,' Bloor said ironically.

Rogers snorted his disbelief. 'More likely jealousy; that he was helping himself on the side.'

There was a clock-ticking silence in the room before Bloor answered. 'Please don't make me angry, Mr Rogers,' he said finally. 'You speak without knowing, and possibly for a good reason, *but please don't.*' Anger and passion were already in him, palpable to a surprised Rogers.

'I'm sorry,' he apologized, meaning it. 'A misdirected comment.'

'You'll have to believe me on this.' Bloor's anger had subsided as quickly as it had risen. 'I'm sure I would never have touched Harriet – whom I respected – if I'd thought that Stoner had had his pig's snout even sniffing at her underwear. I knew Harriet; I knew – almost knew – what made her tick. She detested Stoner as much as I believe she detested her husband of whom she was scared almost witless.' He grimaced as if at some unpleasant recall. 'I asked her once why she stayed with a man she so disliked and she said – and I believed her – that he would kill her should she try to leave him. I asked her what if Stoner told his brother that he suspected me of making love to her and she said that that was something which couldn't possibly happen. My opinion was, and is, that she had something terribly damaging against Stoner or her husband that required them to keep her on a short leash. Don't ask me what that was for I don't know and she never hinted at it.'

Bloor combed fingernails through his beard, occupied in thinking while Rogers waited. 'If I've suggested that Harriet flaunted herself, then I've rather exaggerated what she was doing. Does it make sense for me to have thought that here was a well-educated girl, married to a pig-ignorant lout if his brother was anything to go by, a girl who made herself much too cheap with overdone make-up and going around with Tom, Dick and Harry? And, of course, with Harris Bloor,' he added self-admonitorily.

'Well, thank God that's not yet a crime like smoking almost is,' Rogers said extravagantly. 'What was Harriet's reaction to your cutting your cables, so to speak?'

Bloor looked surprised. 'Nothing spectacular. I'd already told her about the fracas between Stoner and myself – she said she was sorry about that, but it was none of her doing – and that I thought a parting for a while might be better for us both. She apparently thought so too, so it was no big deal.'

'Did she ever tell you anything about her husband?'

'Only by implication that he was a cruel, unloving and lying bastard.'

'That must be quite a few wives' opinion of their husbands,' Rogers said cynically. 'What about the unfortunate Henry Fowler who presumably took your place? What do you know about him?'

'Nothing. He's on the head keeper's staff and fairly new here. Certainly less than four months.'

And not wasting any time either, Rogers thought. Waiting to see if there was anything more to be volunteered, each man staring calmly at the other, and finding there was nothing, he pushed back his chair and stood.

'I'm grateful,' he said amiably as if they were old friends. 'You've been most helpful.'

He wasn't out of the room by a few feet before pawing in his pocket for his pipe and tobacco and wondering at his fortitude in surviving so long without them.

In his car, partially anaesthetized by nicotine, he mulled over what had been said and not said. Despite Bloor's angry rejection of it, he still thought that there was the possibility of Stoner having been one of his sister-in-law's lovers. In his experience of women as a police officer he knew that a fair proportion of them – refined and unrefined, educated and uneducated alike – were not too often averse to what was called the rough stuff; reputedly the enormously equipped, often uncouth, sweaty T-shirt lovers.

## 8

Rogers, returning to the service gate area, saw with relief, tempered by a settled apprehension that somehow someone would have buggered things up in his absence, that the car which was the coffin of its grisly occupants had been removed to the Headquarters garage for its detailed examination; the bodies almost certainly transferred to the mortuary for Dr Twite to perform on in his cavalier version of anatomizing. The yellow boundary tapes had been removed and the park gates opened. The Major Incident coach – more generally referred to by the CID as the Murder Wagon – was in business and parked, ill-advisedly, in the growing heat of the sun.

The coach, from which the seats had been removed to allow the installation of small offices for presumably badly stunted police personnel, had been built with comfort taking second place. Entering it, in the sense that he was now taking over, Rogers checked that an adequate staff had been supplied. Not wholly with enthusiasm, he found that he had WPS Magnolia Flowers as a collator of incoming information. By repute, her sweetness of temperament and her possession of huge shirt-straining breasts were believed to provoke mental and physical anguish in those of her male colleagues feeling tempted to respond to either, and then inevitably being charged with sexual harassment. Rogers, happily immune to any fascination with sweetness in women with or without overlarge fleshy upholstery, could view either in passing as part of the décor.

A PS Hamish Black from Administration – he was a one-time bank cashier – was to handle matters of petty finance, overtime and any necessary feeding of the troops; a WPC McAdam to manage the radio console and to keep a log of messages; and two otherwise unwanted PCs to act as bodies-in-waiting to do things not already thought of. It wasn't much, but Rogers supposed enough, for by recent general standards the apparent killing of a couple in coitus hadn't been assessed as a high grade investigation as would be the killing of a politician or member of a pop group, or a serial killing.

Rogers's on-the-scene office was a telephone booth-sized cabinet containing a 24x18 inch metal table with a tray for his papers and a last year's copy of the *Police Almanac*. The metal chair, which didn't quite accommodate his fairly standard-sized buttocks and forced him into an almost crouched position, was unyieldingly unupholstered. The contained atmosphere in the office could have baked bread, and he sweated.

Fishing through the meagre input of documents left in the tray, he read and initialled a helpful report from DC Connors who had obtained statements from two residents in a clump of farm cottages close to the perimeter of the Knoll Wood side of the park.

One was from an elderly Mrs Himes who, in bed and reading at about half-past ten – though she naturally wasn't too sure of the time – had heard the sound of a man's voice – she thought he was shouting – followed by what she took to be a gun being fired and the screaming of one of the park's peacocks which she thought was being killed. It could, she had said, have been a woman screaming, though she couldn't be sure and didn't wish to think that it had been. It was, she had said on being questioned further, the only gun she had heard being fired that night. It definitely came from the park and not from Knoll Wood which was behind her house and the park and from where she had heard shots at night on occasions in the past.

The second was from an employee of the farm, a Charlie Benham, who said he was in his outside shed with the door open and building a model ship which was his hobby. At what he thought to be between ten thirty and eleven o'clock, he heard a man shouting something angry from not too far inside the park, followed by a gunshot from what he judged to be a sporting shotgun. Then there was a frightened woman screaming, or what he then thought to be that, until he realized it could have been one of the park's peacocks which often made a nuisance of themselves though he wasn't about to complain of course. He had heard no shots either before or after this when he went to bed at one o'clock. He had heard gunshots at night before, but these always came from Knoll Wood where there had been a lot of poaching. Now that he knew of the murders he was deeply sorry that he hadn't telephoned the police, but at the time he hadn't taken it all that seriously. Not two murders in a place like the safari park.

Finished with the paperwork, Rogers called in Inspector Hassell – he was convinced, almost convinced, that Hassell was improperly interested in Flowers's bodily excesses, but good luck to him in his endeavours if they were the focus of his dangerous ambitions – who told him that he had returned the squad of PCs to Headquarters and that the down-on-the-knees search had produced nothing more than that which was contained in a small polythene bag held by Sergeant Flowers. This, in his, Hassell's, opinion was worth sod-all, with which, on Rogers having it brought to him for examination, he agreed.

Hassell also told him that the head keeper of the park, a Mr Harry Halcro – a peevish Mr Halcro – had called at the Murder Wagon seeking him out, looking not too pleased about his absence and saying that he would be calling back on a matter of some importance when he definitely expected the superintendent to be there.

'It isn't', growled Rogers in his irritation, 'as if I've been sitting on my backside all morning, and I'd have got around to seeing him this afternoon anyway.'

He was on the telephone trying to raise Lesley Wing when a hugely moist Flowers looked in through his door and said that Mr Halcro was approaching and obviously intent on seeing him. Glad of any reason for getting out of his parboiling smoke-filled mini-office, he emerged from the coach as Halcro brought his buggy to a halt – it was fitted with side-screens and had been enamelled a matt elephant grey – and unfolded his beanpole height from it.

Apart from being tall and appearing to be in his early sixties, he had a swarthily gaunt, deeply ridged and fissured face, and a veinous nose. Not too far from looking like a sad bloodhound with dragged-down eye pouches in loose skin, he had fierce bushy eyebrows and grizzled hair. He wore carelessly a non-uniform green twill jacket with stained beige trousers. Rogers thought him rough enough to scratch matches on.

He walked to him and held out his hand, having it grasped in a grip more suited to crushing beer cans. 'Morning, Mr Halcro,' he said affably. 'I'm Rogers and you've been looking for me.'

Halcro nodded unsmilingly. 'I have,' he said in a voice like the sound of sawing wood, manifestly annoyed. 'I thought you'd be chasing me up; at least about my chap Fowler.'

'I'd have got to you eventually,' Rogers told him, unruffled, largely pacified by being out of the hotbox coach and in the shade of a huge beech tree. 'You do know of what happened, I imagine? And how?'

Halcro nodded, not overly appeased. 'I do, though the world's full of death by one way or another. We all go eventually so I don't brood too long over any that don't involve me personally.' He shrugged his *memento mori* off, still irritated, but calming down. 'I'm here to find out if you know about the gun.'

Rogers frowned, all affability fled. 'I don't, but I'm sure you're about to tell me.'

Surprisingly Halcro smiled; it looked a sombre smile though with an abundance of teeth. 'I thought you'd be interested,' he said, 'although I'm bloody furious about it happening to me. My chap was shot, is that right?' Seeing Rogers's cautious nod, he asked, 'Do you know with what?'

'Without spreading it around unnecessarily, I thought he'd been killed by a shotgun; possibly a single-barrelled one.'

Halcro was sombre now. 'You've got it right there, superintendent, and I'm sure it'll be by one of the single-shot Ithaca guns I keep in my office. When I heard about Henry being found shot dead with Mrs Stoner . . .' – his mention of her name reflected displeasure in his face – '. . . I checked on the armoury cupboard and found one was missing.'

'One of how many?'

'Three. We keep them for emergencies with the larger animals, though while I've been here the need hasn't arisen.'

'From a locked cupboard? Forcing it?'

Halcro grimaced, his face all creases and sagging eye pouches. 'No. I've slipped up there. I trusted too much the security of my office for there's no access to anyone else but staff.'

'With the inevitable result,' Rogers said caustically. 'Cartridges as well, I imagine?'

'Yes, but harmless in the main. They are birdshot cartridges, number eights I think they're called; or sometimes dust shot. But there were a few standard cartridges as necessary alternatives if things escalated, you understand. One or two of either could have been taken without being missed.'

'Just that I know you had them,' Rogers said, not at all sympathetically and shaking his head. 'Easily available for someone to take and blow some poor bugger's head off. In this case one of your own staff.'

'I know that already, so you don't have to damned well rub it in.' He had become defensively aggressive.

'No, I don't,' Rogers agreed, 'but it is a bit naughty to be careless with guns. If I were you I'd be ready to expect visits from one of my Scenes of Crime men and an unfriendly somebody at my Headquarters interested in the proper security of firearms. Have you reported it to Mrs Wing?'

'Not yet. I thought you first, obviously.'

'And rightly,' Rogers agreed. He paused for a moment, then said, 'Tell me about Henry Fowler. All that you can.' The thought of him brought back inescapably to his reluctant mind his torn and bloody face.

With his regenerated need for nicotine worrying itself at his nerve endings, he refilled his pipe and lit it, blowing smoke into the green effulgence of leaves above him.

Following Rogers's lead, Halcro retrieved a cheroot – it resembled a piece of tarry rope – from an inner pocket of his jacket and lit it with a gas lighter. 'I've not a lot,' he said. 'In fact I've hardly got to know the man. Mr Wimbush hired him over my head and he would have all his personal details.'

'And he's away.'

'Yes, he is.' Halcro quite clearly wasn't about to discuss his employer.

'Tell me what he was like for the time he was here. There must be something.'

'He's been employed here since the middle of May – say just over three months – and he helps out with the elephants and rhinos. He seems to know what he's doing, having done something similar in a wildlife park near Haughton-le-Swale, though out of it for several years.' He stopped, probably thinking that was enough.

'You knew nothing more of his background?'

'No, but I probably would have when Mr Wimbush came back. He never spoke about himself and he's here as an unmarried man.'

'You knew that he and Mrs Stoner were friendly? Perhaps a little over-friendly?' Smelling the rankness of the smoke from Halcro's cheroot, he was being driven to believing he might be ready to support any move to ban cheroots from public use.

'We're speaking in confidence, are we?' Halcro asked warily.

'Completely,' Rogers assured him.

'Well, speak no ill of the dead unless one has to, but Mrs Stoner went through most of my male staff like a brush fire.'

Rogers smiled and, while watching his eyes, said jokingly, 'Excluding yourself of course?' then laughing as if at the wholly laughable unlikely.

The ageing Halcro could have been receiving a compliment and he guffawed. 'Be your age, man. Would I be telling you this if I was one of them?' There was nothing in his eyes to be construed as alarm or a guilty knowledge. 'You'd understand I couldn't prove any of this in a court of law, even if they'd got me there and believed I'd said it to you.'

With an understanding between them mutually accepted, Rogers said, 'Tell me what you know about Fowler's character, his personality. So far, I don't have too clear a picture of him.'

'I haven't either,' Halcro admitted. 'In three months it'd be a mite difficult to know anyway. He was a good worker and got on well with the man who was fitting him in. He was a friendly sort of cove; mixing with the others when he could and showing an interest in them and in what they did. I'd say quite secretive about himself though; cagey, you know.'

64

'Running away from a wife? Owing money to someone?'

Halcro nodded. 'That sort of thing.'

'Hmm. Your chap Coope's been mentioned in despatches. Gets around at night chasing moths, I'm told.'

Halcro made a sound in his throat that could have been a derisive laugh. 'Yes, he's known as Mothy Coope. He's a temporary, also fitted in by Mr Wimbush. Just left school and waiting to go to university.' He laughed again. 'You're asking me about him and Mrs Stoner, I suppose?'

'The question was in my asking,' Rogers said. 'I'm told he lodges with you.'

Halcro snapped his lighter at his evil-smelling cheroot that had died on him while he talked. 'In a way he does, though in the annexe and not in the house. He's only eighteen and a good lad; well-meaning, but still wet around the ears. While I'm not certain, though it's more or less known as true amongst the staff, it seems that Mrs Stoner ambushed him one night when he was collecting his moths, sampled what he had and then later put him to one side as a sort of kindness to the young. Educating him in a sense, if you know what I mean.'

'If I know anything about eighteen-year-old students,' Rogers said cynically, 'they put us very much in the shade and get that sort of experience long before they're thinking of sitting for their A-levels. You're saying that being in your annexe, you've no real control over when he comes in or goes out?'

'That's about it. He's old enough and big enough to look after his own well-being and personal love life.'

'What does he do in terms of earning his keep?'

'A bit of help such as cleaning up here and there; doing odd unskilled chores such as clearing rhino dung . . .' – he showed his teeth at that – '. . . as they crop up. At the moment he's taking an inventory of our wildfowl; flamingos, geese, ducks and coots. It keeps him busy and out of harm's way.'

Rogers looked at his wrist-watch. 'I'd be grateful if you'd have him here at my office . . .' – he indicated the coach with his pipe – '. . . at three o'clock; unbriefed and in his normal state of mind. Nothing of what I question him about will be attributed to you.'

Back in the Murder Wagon, he was told by Flowers that Mrs

Wing had telephoned on the number he had left with her —was there amusement showing in the sergeant's eyes? — asking for his attendance at her office as soon as he had returned and was free.

Before he left, he asked the standing-by Inspector Hassell to get in touch with Headquarters and to recall the squad of PCs he had earlier dismissed and to organize a five-star search of the area around the summerhouse for a single-barrelled shotgun which may have been discarded there immediately after the killings.

Matters, he thought, were progressing though not so far that he would be wanting to buy anybody a double whisky to celebrate it.

9

With the door of the security office guardroom being open and the room unoccupied, Rogers walked into its cooler shade, knocked on the inner door signboarded *Chief Security Officer* and heard Lesley's voice calling for whoever it was to come in.

She was pinning a printed paper on a wall notice-board when he entered and she turned, smiling at him. 'I'm glad you could come. Were you about to sign off for lunch?'

'It had occurred to me,' he said. 'Join me, will you?'

He took in the office, this not occupying much more time than it took for her to answer him. His first impression was of disciplined green rows of tall foliage and climbing plants paraded against the white skirting boards and on window-sills, then a desk with a telephone, wire trays stuffed with papers, an orange jar of ball pens and coloured pencils; a tall frosted-glass vase of white flowers and a standing photograph frame of which he could only see the back and which he knew would at some time engage his interest. A smallish leather executive chair stood askew behind her desk and within hand's reach was a table holding on it a small radio console. Two PVC-padded wooden chairs and a cupboard-cum-bookcase stood on the highly polished parquet flooring. The room, which held in it an air of military precision, had the sun shining brassily through its two opened windows and smelled of a woman's scent and wax polish.

'Thank you,' she said, 'but I think you'd find it difficult and inconvenient in our restaurant, if that was your intention. The food's very ordinary and touristy anyway.' She was holding dark-eyed his gaze. 'I had arranged a sandwich and coffee lunch for us in my apartment if you'd like that?'

'I would indeed, and I'm grateful,' he replied, wondering happily if this was the thin edge of an attractive wedge. Though trying not to read too much into it, he had a highly coloured imagining of their having a drink or two as an aperitif and then both thinking to hell with the sandwiches and coffee . . .

'Could we first have a few words here on a couple of developments?' he suggested. It was an opening he intended stretching into a more lengthy interview. His work always came first, depending on what one meant by 'first'.

'Of course.' She moved to her desk and sat. 'Can you manage with the visitors' chair?'

Seated to one side of her, he said, 'Quentin Coope, a temporary keeper here and apparently mad on moths, has been named to me as somebody about whom you should have some interesting information.'

'Ah.' She pursed her lips as though there was an initial reluctance to speak about him. 'Since he started working here he's certainly been seen wandering the park at all hours of the night, though never checked by us in the security sense. Toby Wimbush knows of his interest in entomology and has not only authorized his employment, but his night collecting activities as well, though naturally only outside the animal enclosures and compounds. My staff do come across him at all hours, but no entries are made in the Report Book.'

She laughed, almost inaudibly. 'They believe he's daft, of course, but he's simply schoolboyishly enthusiastic about moths that appear only to come out at night. You know he's a university undergraduate-in-waiting?'

'Yes, he's also eighteen and hardly a schoolboy. Still, I am told he's a decent young chap.' Rogers held her gaze and asked, 'Would you know if there's any truth in the suspicion that he has at least once fallen to Harriet's attraction?'

'I would be terribly surprised,' she said, though visibly not having been, her face unrevealing of it.

Probably poker-faced like me, Rogers thought, while accepting she had every right to be. 'I've pretty good grounds for believing that it happened at least once.'

'I'm still surprised,' she insisted. 'I hadn't known he was even suspected of it. He's never seemed the type to me, and Harriet had never hinted that she'd been out with him.'

'I'm told it happened one night when his interest should have been focused on his moths.' When Lesley seemed disinclined to take that further, he said, 'The other matter is about a shotgun missing from the armoury cupboard in the head keeper's office. I understand it hasn't yet been reported to you, though it will be.' He was fidgeting in his need for a smoke, only the telling absence of an ashtray in the room holding him back.

She had definitely been surprised at what he said. Surprised and considerably annoyed it seemed, perhaps even at him for having been the bearer of unwelcome news. 'I *haven't* been told, and I damned well should have been. This is from Harry Halcro, I assume?'

'Yes. He discovered it only this morning.'

'Are you about to suggest it was used to kill Henry Fowler?'

'I can only guess it was. And, of course, it's still missing.'

She thought about that, looking with narrowed eyes through the window nearest to her. 'How did it go missing?' she asked. 'By breaking open the cupboard?'

'Apparently not.' He now had to be careful. 'I'm sorry, I don't wish to be uncooperative, but Halcro will be seeing you shortly and he'll no doubt give you the full details.' He paused, thinking something was becoming strained between them, then said, pushing on with it, 'I don't suppose you've had any previous reports from him about the misuse of the guns he holds in his office?'

'Nothing,' she answered him, a little stiffly. 'I would have told you before had there been.'

'I'm sure you would,' he hastened to assure her. 'It's just that I have to put a direct question to you about it.' Almost apologetically, he said, 'There are one or two further questions I have while I'm about it. Mr Latouche; he has a slight accent I can't place. Is he something other than English?'

She stared at him for several seconds, started to say something, then appeared to change her mind and said, 'I've been told he comes from South Africa – Cape Town, I believe – though he was born in England of French parents and educated here. His father's a veterinarian in Cape Town and he, Jacques, is here on an exchange scheme of sorts.'

She was silent again, manifestly thinking hard. 'He'd be most annoyed if he knew I'd been talking about him behind his back. He really is a sensitive man.'

'More to the point, you feel he's nobody I need concern myself with? Nobody likely to dash around shooting people or battering them to death?' It wasn't idle humour from him, for he was watching her reactions very closely.

She laughed easily, free from whatever angst she had appeared to momentarily suffer. 'He's a sweetie, almost certainly immune to women like Harriet and you needn't concern yourself with him.' She laughed again. 'At least, not unless you suspect you are suffering from something like canine hardpad or epizootic lymphangitis.'

'I don't think either.' He smiled, thinking she seemed to be rather defensively friendly about the good-looking Latouche, possibly having something of a crush on him with his possession of a delicacy of manner and his cream hair. 'I accept your opinion of him,' he said, pushing the unwanted thought to one side, 'but is there anything else about him I should know?'

'Nothing you *should*, but if it helps him at all he loves animals to what you might call excess and he does suffer badly over reported cruelties to them. He has what he calls a proper regard for people, but doesn't necessarily like them – he thinks not an uncommon trait. All his words, George; not mine.'

'And mine as well, up to a point,' he said, and meaning it.

'You were going to ask me more about Harriet, were you?' She took a sheet of paper from a tray and put it in front of her. 'My *aide-mémoire*,' she said, 'because I do have a hole or two in my head.'

'It's been trembling on my tongue,' he told her. 'There's more?'

'If I haven't mentioned it before,' she said, 'I feel that underneath a rather superficial flashiness she was a deeply sad and unhappy woman. I know little about the psychology of such a condition, but on thinking about her since this morning, it could be that she was working out whatever neuroses she had by seducing – if she did – any available and willing man with whom she came in contact.'

'What I've been missing,' Rogers murmured, necessarily to himself. Aloud, he asked, 'Would an unhappy woman do that?'

'Most spectacularly,' she assured him. 'And why not?'

He shrugged his bafflement at why so many of her sex succumbed so readily to the illogical. 'Why not indeed,' he agreed diplomatically.

'Yes or no,' she said, returning the paper to her tray, 'there was that edge of darkness to her and it seemed to drive her into cheapening herself with men. Still, all that was before it became obvious from the circumstance of her death that she had probably found in Henry what she might have been looking for.'

She grimaced; a quite attractive moist-mouthed grimace in Rogers's opinion. 'She could be cruel, you know, in a thoughtless way; not accepting that she could hurt badly whoever she was going with by dropping him suddenly for another who had taken her liking.'

This one-time lieutenant in Her Majesty's Armed Forces was, Rogers considered, much too bloody attractive for what was in effect a rest period for his sometimes over-the-top mating instincts. It didn't help that Angharad periodically haunted his mind, enough anyway to be a warning red light against an ill-judged infidelity.

'You've more on Harriet?' he asked, pushing things carnal to one side.

'Nothing of use to you,' she said, 'except probably this.' She slid open an upper drawer of her desk and reached into it, handing to him a coloured photograph. 'That', she told him, 'is Harriet with Queenie, our lioness. You may keep it if you wish.'

The photograph was of a young, fairly ordinary-looking woman – definitely not Rogers's type because, as with Sergeant Flowers, she possessed breasts of an intimidating amplitude – seated on grass with an arm around the neck of an adult lioness the colour of her hair. It appeared to him that if there was any unusual attractiveness about her, it was of the fluffy soft-as-marshmallow sort. He would look at her later under magnification, but for the moment he preferred the lioness.

'A courageous woman,' he said. 'Does Queenie allow anyone to be so familiar?'

'I think Harriet was an exception.' For some reason his question or the look on his face had amused her. 'It was taken for a publicity campaign.'

'Say', he put to her, 'that Harriet and Fowler were killed with the motive being a murderous jealousy or something similar. The question then would be, *why* when she was being made love to by Fowler, and not when she had been presumably known to have been doing the same thing with other men?'

She thought about that. 'I see your point, but we'd have to know for sure that the someone who did it actually knew what was going on with Harriet. And, as importantly, where, unless she used the summerhouse as a routine meeting place.'

'I'm sure you're right,' he agreed with her, 'and I'm grateful. Before we leave I have to tell you that David Lingard will be searching her room later this afternoon. I'd be happy if you could be with him when he does. It'd be helpful to have your views on what we might find there.'

She nodded. 'Of course I will. He'll be getting in touch?'

'He will,' he assured her, then adding, 'There is a further question I'd forgotten. Do you mind?'

'Not too terribly,' she answered, which meant to him that she did rather.

'I'm sorry, but I do have to see the unpleasant Stoner again. Would you brief me on where he would have been, or where he was supposed to have been, at eleven o'clock last night?'

'I know precisely,' she told him. 'He would be, or should be, at his half-hourly contact which is Point B at the public access gate near the restaurant on the south side of the park.'

'Where would he go from there?'

'To Point D in the vicinity of the gas incinerator.'

'Is that anywhere near the summerhouse?'

She pursed her lips. 'Near enough I suppose as the crow flies, but not to get to unless you are one. You'd have to retrace your steps a long way to get to it.'

He grimaced. 'And Stoner isn't a crow either, of course. What about the much more pleasant Harris Bloor at four o'clock this morning?'

'He too should be, or would be, at his half-hourly Point A at the service entrance gate.'

'Where is that in relation to the gate where the bodies were found?'

'That's the service exit gate and it's on the opposite side of the park, as far from the entrance gate as you can get.'

'Assuming Bloor was at his point, could he hear a car moving towards the exit gate?'

She pursed her lips, shaking her head. 'Seriously, I'd doubt it. It would be about a thousand yards away from him with trees, animal housing and enclosures in between. He would definitely be able to hear whatever traffic might be passing on the public road, but I'm sure he wouldn't confuse this with any traffic moving inside the park.'

'And the position of the summerhouse in all this? About midway?'

She shook her head. 'No. Nearer the service exit gate where the bodies were found.'

'What do you think', he said, pushing it a little further, 'might be the reason for . . .'

He stopped as the telephone on Lesley's desk rang and she reached for it. 'Lesley Wing here,' she answered crisply, then, 'Yes, I'll hand you over to him.' Passing the receiver to him, she said, 'Sergeant Flowers.'

He took it from her, listening to what Flowers said while he hid an extreme annoyance behind his professional non-expression. She had received a message from Assistant Chief Constable Pitt-Bowsher – Rogers's unfavourite immediate superior and a largish thorn in his flesh – that he, Superintendent Rogers, was to drop whatever he was doing and return to Headquarters, there to report to the ACC's office. This was to be considered a matter of the utmost importance, of extreme urgency, and to be acted on at once.

To Rogers, it sounded like serious trouble brewing for someone, nastily ominous in the way the message was couched; it usually foreshadowed no good at all for any officer ordered to report personally without a supporting explanation.

Having been living a recent life of what he thought to be an above average rectitude – which was not much of a defence anyway – he had few worries about himself, but was prepared to be bloody-minded whatever.

He stood, his underclothing unsticking from him – he thought almost audibly – and said, 'I'm sorry, Lesley. A Purple One order back to barracks. Something's come up, probably not about this job, and Higher Authority sounds as if it's panicking. Another time for the sandwiches, perhaps? Or, if I'm still in good health, a meal in Thurnholme this evening?' He trailed off, suspecting that that might be a non-starter anyway.

While there was a fleeting expression on her face which could mean that she didn't like it, she said, 'Another day, George, and I'll hold you to it.'

Outside it was still cloudlessly hot and he was so irritated about Pitt-Bowsher that he forgot to fill and light his pipe, his usual panacea against the vagaries of life; and this time because of the seemingly ominous change of course promised in his handling of the investigation.

By now, he had decided that Lesley could be potent with

apparently unsatisfied sexuality, something not easily resist-
ible by an uncomplicated man. It did nothing to console him
in his feeling that she might have gone off him; whether, in
fact, she had ever been for him.

# 10

Detective Chief Inspector Lingard had dash; what he
would call – even in his modesty – panache; the kind associated with rakish sports cars and rangy women who were
high-flyers in industry or the arts and who knew that they
were a little more than the equal of the men with whom they
chose to associate.

With more money than he needed in his present job – he
had sold his much-loved but badly failing veteran Bentley for
an unexpected small fortune – and with Rogers apparently
intending to hang on to his superintendentship for ever,
Lingard was considering seriously a transfer to the Metropoli-
tan Police. As an intending lifelong bachelor he could
then apply his talents to the obtaining of a lengthy tour of
duty as a bodyguard to one of the junior or lesser royals and
travel.

Before setting out for Crouch Aughton – it was in a different
police area – in his recently acquired and much less expensive middle-aged Bentley drophead coupé with which he
had yet to fall in love, he had checked the town's provenance
in a gazetteer for whatever he could milk from it. There was
little of note other than that it contained unhelpfully a number of now defunct cotton mills, that it was reputed to have
been the birthplace of an eleventh-century Danish king,
Swegn the Bastard, and that it had in fact the ruins of a
Roman temple dedicated to the goddess Vesta, complete
with the once walled-in bones of what must have been a
wayward Vestal anything-but-a-Virgin. None of which,
Lingard considered, would help his enquiry in a town which

had undoubtedly died an industrial death on the far side of the Great Morte Moor and a fairish drag even in his Bentley.

Entering it on this sweatingly hot day with the car's hood down, he was not surprised to find it on the dreary side with a single brownstone church, garishly appointed shops and stores, generous on red paint and chromium plate, and an acre or two of a half-occupied industrial estate.

The local police were fortunate in not having been architecturally restructured as had Lingard's force, their Divisional Headquarters occupying an attractive Georgian stone mansion, relic of a long dead Cotton Master, with a pillared entrance to a civilized reception hall which didn't smell of the last meal cooked in the canteen.

Detective Inspector Whincut, deputed by his superintendent to accommodate the enquiries of the visiting Lingard, was cheerfully extrovert about problems occurring in another officer's bailiwick and therefore unlikely to tax his professional concern.

While Lingard sat opposite him with a mug of vile-tasting sugared coffee cooling at his side, occasionally charging his sinuses with Macouba snuff – his first reserve tranquillizer – Whincut told him that he knew William Albert Stoner, a thick-headed and violent bastard if there was ever one. He had what were now written-off juvenile convictions for two separate thefts of suitcases from the local railway station, and a service conviction for bunging it in on an unfortunate Wren. There were no other convictions as an adult recorded against him and Whincut took the opportunity of remarking what a useless bloody security guard he must be.

Stoner, it appeared, had been on the receiving end of a cruel bashing by his brother Laurence a couple of years back, and, having made his complaint to the police, had withdrawn it a day or two later. If Lingard was looking for the murderer of Harriet and her boyfriend – whoever that daft bugger might be – then he thought he need look no further than William Albert who was, he again commented, unfitted to be any kind of a security guard.

Whincut had also had dealings with Laurence Stoner – who was also known under the aliases Charles Forbes Oakes and Charles Mountstevens – apparently a cut above his brother and, criminality excluded, as different from him as a reasonably civilized man is supposed to be from a subnormal baboon. Stoner was at present doing a well-deserved sentence of three years' imprisonment – and serve the bugger right – for his fraudulent involvement with council building contracts in collusion with a local borough councillor; that had been dealt with by the force's Fraud Squad and he, thank God, had had very little to do with it himself.

Interestingly enough, he said, that conniving and slippery sod Laurence was now on the tail-end of his three-year sentence and serving it in Hardenhuish Open Prison, no more than six miles away; that had to be a bloody fix if there was ever one. It was never far enough away, he complained in a spasm of bitterness, because all the bastards inside, well most of them anyway, were more or less allowed to treat the so-called prison as a home-from-home with visits to Crouch Aughton serving as an occasional leisure and shopping centre. He admitted though that they generally behaved in a more civilized manner than the shaven-headed, ear-ring-wearing, split-jeans-trousered, pig-ignorant yobbos living here in the town; a bloody disgrace to the few decent and honest citizens left there.

Asked by Lingard, who had suffered his law and order onslaught without blinking, what Laurence Stoner did for a living when not in prison, Whincut said with derision in his voice that only God would know, but he did call himself an entrepreneur, believed to be dealing in, among other things, agricultural machinery such as damn great combine harvesters stolen from other parts of the country which were then tarted up and disguised and shipped abroad. But he'd never admit that, naturally.

A clever chap, Lingard had murmured, so what about Harriet whose unmarried name was Gager?

Whincut said with reproach in his voice that he hadn't forgotten and he had checked on her. She was the daughter of a local physiotherapist who had then apparently gone off to join the French Foreign Legion or something similar in disgust on her leaving home at a highly sexed sixteen or thereabouts and then living with Laurence Stoner. She had, in fact, been charged with her husband – or whatever he was to her – and the bent councillor, though only on a single count of conspiracy. And that went out of the window even before the case went to the jury.

Apart from that and the gross error in her shacking up with one of the Stoners – a notorious family – there was nothing recorded against her and, no, he hadn't the slightest idea of why the usually cunning and despicable Laurence would send her to be looked after – ha, ha! – by the equally despicable William Albert.

No, he had replied after Lingard's last question, prior to his arrest Laurence had rented a room at the Metropol Hotel here and, so far as he knew or cared, he had not visited the hotel or any of his pre-prison haunts in the town.

And, yes, he would telephone the governor of Hardenhuish Prison – if he might be excused for calling it a prison – and arrange for Lingard's interview with Stoner; should Stoner, of course, give his gracious consent to be interviewed.

In the meantime, the hospitable Whincut had asked, would Lingard give him the pleasure of joining him for a scratch lunch in the mess? Lingard, whose idea of a lunch wasn't one begat in the frying pans of any normal police canteen, accepted with thanks though knowing that his educated stomach would most probably later regret it; or, even, reject it on somebody's carpet.


# 11


The building that was signposted reasonably discreetly as *H. M. Prison, Hardenhuish* looked to Lingard like a smallish redbrick manor house not yet old enough to have a

Virginia creeper clothe its walls or lichen blotch its pedimented blue-slate roof. With no suggestion of bars at its windows, its spacious rhododendron-planted grounds encircled by a mockery of a fence, it looked, as Whincut's complaining suggested, as if it had been taken over by a four star hotel.

Parking his Bentley in as conspicuous a place as he could against possible theft, he was shown into a friendly-mannered governor's office. After a few words with him – he could have been taken for an Anglican vicar wearing off-duty and out-of-season hairy tweeds – he learned that Stoner had already been informed of his wife's death. 'Poor man,' he had said, 'he's taken it extremely hard,' then had had him led by a warder in mufti to what was obviously a well-furnished sitting-room, though described as a room for the visits of the prisoners' relatives and friends.

Stoner was standing at one of the open windows when Lingard was ushered in, introduced and left to it. He turned and greeted the detective with an undertaker's gravity, his hand outstretched to be shaken; Lingard, surprised, took it.

'I appreciate your coming to see me,' Stoner said. 'I really do.'

While observing the formalities, one of which was Lingard's production of his warrant card and Stoner's reading it carefully, the detective was committing to memory the man's externals, reasonably certain indicators of what made him tick.

Even to a quite discerning assessment the decently articulated voice could be warm and friendly, coming from an oddly theatrically mannered man as tall and elegant as Lingard himself and as leanly alert as a highly bred racehorse. His wavy hair, trimmed in a style that was never perfected by a prison barber, was a dark auburn, glossy with good living. His light grey eyes held Lingard's sometimes daunting blue ones in a searching stare, his nose prominent and thin in the sunken-cheeked ascetic face of a man who didn't overeat, his mouth wide and showing a leaning to humour, his jaws strong.

He wore a light fawn jacket and off-white narrow trousers, both manifestly tailored by somebody who knew his stuff and matched with a darker tan shirt and a blue and gold striped tie.

Most meeting him for the first time and unwise enough to trust their own eyes would be impressed, though in this Lingard allowed himself to go only part of the way. And he knew that he would not be surprised were not women immediately attracted to him. Finally, Lingard could see no signs of his being too crushed either by his wife's terrible death or by his being the inmate of a prison.

With his hand released, Lingard took out his tiny ivory box, pinched a generous inhalation of snuff, and said, 'In a way, it appears that I've been sent here unnecessarily. Your brother's already told you?'

'He telephoned the governor this morning.' He cocked what could be a whimsical eyebrow were he not supposed to be smitten by bereavement. 'May I say that I'm surprised you were sent, in effect, to deliver a message I'd have thought better done by a much lesser rank than yours. A detective chief inspector, in fact! I suspect there's more, of course?'

'Your wife was murdered,' Lingard pointed out, believing he was about to have a spot of bother in getting any sort of an interview from a particularly cool character.

'I telephoned William back, which is one of the amenities allowed us,' Stoner said. 'He told me, and he had little choice, that my dear Harriet had been killed in the arms of a lover. A male lover, thank God, and nothing to bring too much discredit on herself. So what else have you come to see me about?'

'Your brother primarily.' Lingard took more snuff, his last noseful not having done much for him. 'Even conceding that he had suffered a sort of bereavement and, presumably, a shock, his refusal to answer pertinent questions about your wife's identity or to give your home address needed some explaining.'

'It does?' Stoner sounded overly polite.

'I'm sure so. The latter, of course, we now know to have been an understandable discretion, your being here in durance vile if I may put it like that.' Lingard smiled with his mouth shut, then added, 'Then there's the matter of sending your wife into your brother's care and protection. Those sort of inexplicabilities.'

Stoner moved back to the open window and with a quite studied lack of haste took a flat red packet from a jacket pocket, slid out a cigarette and put it between his lips. Putting a flame to it from a gas lighter he blew smoke out through the window.

'There are', he said conversationally and not too seriously, 'very few rules in this establishment. In particular, one does not commit buggery with a fellow inmate without the written consent of the governor, or, more inconveniently, smoke in this visitors' reception room even with it. I very naturally try to obey them . . .' – he grinned hugely, apparently forgetting his bereavement – '. . . but there are occasions when the devil drives.'

'Not being answers to my questions,' Lingard said smoothly, 'my particular devil will be needing something more serious than what you've so far given me.'

Stoner flapped a hand at one of the bloated easy chairs. 'Do sit down – I'd like to call you David if I may – and I promise I'll join you after I've finished this cigarette. In the meantime I shall fill you in, as you policemen say, with what I believe you've come for.'

Lingard sat, wondering if he would ever get the opportunity to lead the interview, at the moment agreeing to wait – though suffering it ungladly – and see and to profit from this man's flippant garrulity, so much like his own at its worst. 'To the point then,' he said, 'and I'm waiting.'

There were sounds of movement from within the house and from above the ceiling a radio broadcast too loudly folk and western music; sounds which Lingard could exclude from his hearing by, in effect, refusing to accept that he could hear them.

Stoner blew more smoke through the window, then leaned

with his back against its sill. 'I'm sorry you have to see me here, David, in as it were the company of fraudulent financiers, of bent – if you'll forgive me – policemen, paedophiliac clergymen and social workers, together with a few not guilty and misunderstood characters such as myself. Mind, I haven't always been so stuffily honest, but I'm telling you the truth, mainly because I see no profit in lying.'

He smiled his all-encompassing no doubt woman-stunning smile. 'First of all, owning as I do to a delicacy of feeling, I don't wish you to believe that I'm William Stoner's brother. I am inflicted with the same name because his mother was the earlier foster mother of me, the unwanted child of a man who seemed to have regarded his fathering of me as a major error, and who has consequently for ever remained unknown to me.'

He wasn't sounding too happy about that. 'My foster mother knew something of his identity, of course, for I was later sent to a private boarding school, obviously paid for by my unknown father. I say this because even now I get cheques from a London solicitor who, bloody-mindedly, refuses either to see me or to answer my letters on the subject, and who says no more than that he has been instructed by an interested party – the tight-lipped bastard let slip once that he was a man of position and wealth – to pay me these fairly handsome amounts. Christ!' he swore. 'He must have had a hairy conscience about me!'

He frowned, drawing at his cigarette and coughing. 'I suppose I'm literally what used to be known as a bastard, though at least with the comforting thought that I didn't come from my foster mother's degraded loins, for she was a dreadfully immoral woman. She hated me as a child, had no reservations about thumping me hard and often and calling me publicly "that 'orrible little bastid". I tell you this because I've a great objection to being known by my better friends as that prick's brother. If I'm anything, I'm his stepbrother, and that's bad enough. He doesn't like me and I don't like him.'

'That didn't stop you sending your wife to him while you were in chokey,' Lingard pointed out, not yet convinced he should be sympathetic, or show signs that he was believing too much of what could be plausible and tarted-up manure.

Stoner smiled; not a friendly smile. 'I really didn't think that I could leave her at home within reach of the indecencies of my friends. William, to the contrary, was frightened of me and she would be safe even in his filthy hands. He was the only man I could trust with her, and then only because he couldn't.'

'He couldn't?' Lingard echoed him.

'He'd been kicked in the balls some years back – and a well-deserved kick it was too – and he'd lost them and any possible use of them to a surgeon's knife.' Stoner was all mock sympathy. 'Poor chap. You have to be sorry for him, don't you? He isn't capable of bedding anyone; so who better?'

'So who better?' Lingard agreed, having been stoical in not flinching in sympathy with the sufferer. 'But what about other men? Such as the one found dead with her? I'm afraid that he and your wife were found very much together, you understand.'

'So I do understand. Look, David,' he said earnestly, 'I can't pretend to be too grief-stricken; that'd be hypocritical. She wasn't my wife and never had been. Nor had we been that way from way back. Not since she screwed her way through any presentable and willing male who lived in Crouch Aughton and all parts east. As I'd more or less snatched her out of her school's fifth form I still believe I've a responsibility for her. I've a feeling for her – not now a sexual one, for I've never taken to sharing it with other men – but she's so damned vulnerable; too generous with what nature's given her and too likeable for her own good. To be frank, David, I think there was a smidgen of nymphomania in her. Poor darling,' he added as a kind of postscript, 'she had so much to give and yet chose to throw it away.'

Lingard would have gone through a minor sort of hell before he would malign a woman he had made love to, as Stoner had done. Not being in the business of discouraging such expressions of a man's dislikes and beliefs, his face reflected nothing but a polite interest. 'Your stepbrother William,' he reminded him. 'He had been married, I understand, being emasculated or not.'

'That was after his marriage and before her death, poor woman. I'm afraid I wasn't a party to how they managed with what they thought necessary for the maintenance of their marriage. I just felt sorry for her anyway.' His eyes seemed to challenge the detective who was recharging his sinuses with Macouba. 'If you're thinking the way I believe you to be, I've to be honest and say I don't think the stupid prick would have the guts to do it. He'd be scared paralytic to even think of harming Harriet. Believe me he would.'

Lingard held Stoner's gaze, letting him read into it what he could. 'You've visited William at the park, naturally?'

'The village, not the park.' He sounded as if he were unusually groping for words. 'There were still matters we had to discuss.'

'Before your imprisonment, of course?' Lingard suggested helpfully. 'Not since?'

'Yes,' he said, a shade of wariness in his voice. 'Of course.'

Lingard brooded on that in silence, then jerked his head as if in recollection. 'I knew there was something,' he said, knowing he had to be careful that this man didn't turn the interview into a discussion of the improbable. 'I do have to ask you to account for your movements last night; covering the hours of, say, nine to twelve?'

There was silence in the room until Stoner, looking surprised, turned and flipped his cigarette stub out through the window. 'My dear chap!' he expostulated. 'For God's sake! Isn't that taking things too far?'

'Not, I feel, far enough,' Lingard said firmly. 'Not with home leave and whatever it is that's called rehabilitation for the offender which I understand entails your mingling with the as yet unimprisoned members of the local community.' He showed his teeth in an encouraging grin. 'Then, of course, there's the well-publicized matter of Her Majesty's prisoners such as yourself being only on scout's honour or something similar not to leave your beds during the hours of darkness. Accepting that, it doesn't need an awful lot of ingenuity for a man to be able to visit places not all that far distant. For the exercise of *cherchez les femmes* I imagine or, more properly, to cohabit briefly with one's wife or girlfriend.'

He smiled encouragingly, a man wishing to be assured of another's good faith. 'I would like to be persuaded that you were innocently tucked up in bed; at least for last night.' He had been watching Stoner intently. Had it been his imagination in seeing the grey eyes shadow at his words?

'Now you're getting outrageously offensive, David, and I thought we were friends of a kind,' Stoner reproached him from behind a further cigarette he had put in his mouth and was lighting. 'I should, I imagine, now tell you that I shall say nothing further without my solicitor being present. You think?'

'But you won't, I'm sure,' Lingard murmured a shade cynically and mostly to himself.

'I don't want to quarrel with you, David, but I'd like to point out that being where I am would make it difficult for me – no, impossible – to have a woman in my bed to swear by all that's holy that I'd never left it all night.' There was mockery in his smile. 'However, there are residential prison officers here who would certainly give evidence that I could never – positively never – have left here while under their unsleeping custodianship. Try them, my dear chap.'

'As if I wouldn't take your word for it,' Lingard lied pleasantly. 'Could I ask if you consider yourself one of the innocent victims of a repressive society in being in chokey?'

Stoner gave him another of his confidence-inducing smiles. 'You're acting the amateur psychologist on me, aren't you, David? I admit I was sailing close to the wind on the council demolition and rebuilding job, but only on the investment side. Better men than I have done worse and got an OBE or an MBE for doing it.'

'I heard you were also working successfully in exporting dodgy farm machinery,' Lingard murmured. 'It's terrible the suspicions that attach themselves to businessmen apparently deserving of better.'

Stoner smiled again. A quite reassuring smile unless it was noted that the eyes were not joining in. 'You've certainly been talking a lot to Austin Whincut, haven't you? I like him, but you should be warned that he's a man of too many foolish fancies.'

He tossed his half-smoked cigarette through the window, stepped towards Lingard and held out his hand. 'It's been a pleasure, David,' he said in unconcealed sarcasm, 'but I do have to go. If you've made me late for lunch I'll never forgive you.'

Even before Lingard had heaved himself to his feet, Stoner was gone from the room, leaving him now to the necessity of putting his bound-to-be-awkward-and-unwelcome questions to the prison officers about any prisoner's likelihood of leaving his no doubt well-appointed room – never a cell for sure – to wander the countryside in relative freedom.

Despite where he was, his Bentley had neither been criminally taken nor had her wheels stolen, and he patted her scaldingly hot rear end affectionately as he might the hindquarters of a well-loved horse. On his way back to his own county he tried to make up his mind about how much or how little truth he might place on what the unnaturally garrulous and certainly untrustworthy Stoner had told him. It would be difficult.


# 12


Rogers didn't like Geoffrey Pitt-Bowsher, the newly appointed Assistant Chief Constable titularly in supervisory charge of the county's crime. Apart from knowing him to be a five-star prick, he considered him a self-serving smoothie transferred from another force in his chase for a promotion from Chief Superintendent, General Duties. Knowing little about the rough edges of criminal investigation he was, unsurprisingly, deemed suitable for overseeing those who did. His blandly held ignorance of it could make Rogers choke on his morning coffee.

It didn't do anything to mollify his unease on entering Pitt-Bowsher's office that he had with him the hugely formidable Chief Superintendent Harold Gamble, Co-ordinator of No. 12 Regional Crime Squad, a criminal investigation unit covering serious cross-county crime and drugs trafficking. The squad would only be concerned with a county's crime – which included murder – after a specific request for assistance by the county concerned.

Rogers knew Gamble, but had never worked with him. He was a balding fat man with small pale grey eyes set in a shiny tight-skinned puce-complexioned face. Abnormally light on his feet for a big man and only superficially jovial, he was known to be slow on the draw with his cigarettes and even slower in making his shout for drinks on social occasions. He was a fair man, but a bit of a bastard in enforcing discipline, earning himself the sobriquet Flash Harry from the bright yellow socks and the yellow bow-tie he sported with his midnight-blue suits.

Their handshake was a fairly neutral one, an unsmiling Gamble appearing to have something weighty on his mind. Rogers took his seat near Pitt-Bowsher's desk – all mahogany and green leather with a multiplicity of drawers – though not as near it as was Gamble, and prepared himself to be defensively aggressive, though in aid of what he had yet to fathom.

Pitt-Bowsher said, 'I'm glad you could make it, Mr Rogers. Mr Gamble is here on a highly confidential matter and I've given him my assurance that we will treat it so and give him every assistance in what he requires.' Turning to Gamble, he said, 'I'll leave you to it, Harold.'

'To the point,' the fat man – now a heavily sweating fat man

– said to Rogers. 'You are investigating the murder of Henry Fowler, an employee of the Castle Caldbeck Wildlife Park; is that so?'

'I am.' Rogers sensed that Gamble was trying to read something from his expression, or lack of it, and he wondered what the hell? 'And of a Mrs Harriet Stoner,' he pointed out.

'Yes, of course, but we could forget Mrs Stoner for the moment.' Gamble was opening up with the faint beginning of an apparently forced geniality. 'Would you mind putting me in the picture? Detailed, if you don't mind.'

'While I'm happy to, this *is* an odd request, and I'd appreciate being told why,' Rogers said. 'I haven't been told that the RCS had been invited in, or needed to be.' He switched his challenging stare to Pitt-Bowsher. 'Had they been?' he asked him tersely.

'Certainly not,' Pitt-Bowsher told the touchy detective, his expression reflecting an inner irritation. 'It's nothing like that.'

'You know we don't work like that,' Gamble protested, 'and I've no intention of sticking my nose into your investigation. Not in the accepted sense, that is,' he qualified, 'as you'll know when you hear me out.'

'I apologize then,' Rogers said. Then, not too happily, he gave Gamble the substance of the finding of the bodies and the enquiries he had already made. It didn't take long, for having had to forgo his lunch and a design or two on Lesley Wing didn't make for chattiness.

Gamble, whose eyes hadn't left Rogers's face, said, 'Don't jump down my throat about this, but have you learned anything about Fowler that's not – well, not straightforward and ordinary? A whisper, perhaps, which seemed of not much significance at the time?'

Rogers frowned. 'Nothing. Nothing that I can recall. I've no doubt I've been lied to, but that's par for the course anyway.'

'Do you feel that you're dealing with a killing attributable to sexual jealousy, revenge or suchlike?'

'On the face of it I could be, though I'm far from being certain. Because Fowler had his trousers opened, and she her skirt off, it isn't necessarily proof that they were killed making love. Nor does anything satisfy me that they were killed together. Though Fowler was certainly shot in the summer-house, she could have been beaten to death anywhere for, so far, there's no evidence that she was ever in there even though she probably was.'

Rogers paused. He badly wanted to smoke, but knew Pitt-Bowsher to be fanatically anti-tobacco and anti everything else likely to make a man reasonably happy. 'What is fact', he continued, 'is that both were together in the boot of Fowler's car; presumably *en route* to being buried or disposed of some-how outside the park before whoever it was proposing to do it ran into trouble with PC Sims. Considering that, faking their having been copulating together would seem to be pointless.'

'What *would* convince you that they were killed having intercourse?' Gamble sounded anxious to want agreement on this.

'Whatever is found by Dr Twite when he does the post-mortem examination this afternoon. If he finds semen that proves a contact between both bodies I shall be satisfied. If Fowler's blood matches that found in the summerhouse, I shall certainly accept that he died there, particularly as there are shot-gun pellets embedded in the wall nearest to the bloodstaining.'

He stared hard at Gamble with darkened eyes, then at Pitt-Bowsher, choosing not to conceal his growing irritation, almost anger. 'Now perhaps somebody can tell me why I'm here being cross-examined about an investigation that's this force's particular business and not that of the Regional Crime Squad.' At this moment, what with the afternoon's oppressive heat and his system's need for food and for nicotine, he didn't much give a bloody damn how either Pitt-Bowsher or Gamble would take it.

There was silence in the office other than for the impinging of remote voices and sounds of movement from offices on the same floor. If Pitt-Bowsher was justifiably affronted, he was too new on the job to show it; Gamble, suddenly snatching deftly at a bluebottle fly circling his sweating face, squeezed it in his fist and dropped its mashed body on to the carpet.

He said, visibly unhappy about something and ignoring Rogers's outburst, 'I hope you're right, because I'm going to tell you why all this no doubt disturbing interference into your investigation. But just one thing more before it slips my mind. Have you had an enquiry made of the Haughton-le-Swale Safari Park to check on his previous employment there?'

Rogers let his bafflement show. 'No, I haven't. That's for when I've managed to catch my breath over more immediate matters. Why do you ask? Is that so important?' He still wasn't happy about things.

'God knows now,' Gamble muttered mostly to himself. 'It's bad enough in all conscience, but when we're referring to your Henry Fowler, we're actually talking about one of my detective sergeants who's working – or was working – under-cover in the park. Not the least of my worries is that his cover may have been blown.'

There were more long moments of clock-ticking silence as Rogers, manifestly under close scrutiny by both men, was adjusting his thinking to this unexpected bombshell of infor-mation. What was he to put first? That a fellow policeman had been murdered; that his seeming carelessness was about to affect adversely Rogers's investigation as an unwanted com-plication? Uncharacteristically, it left him bloody-mindedly angry that this Fowler had been stupid enough, or short-sighted enough, to get himself killed like somebody who didn't quite know what the hell he was doing. And, most probably, when taking time off with a skirtless woman.

'I see,' he said, thinking that his words were inadequate. 'I'm sorry. I couldn't know, of course, and it does make a difference. He was on the job for you, obviously?'

'Yes.' Now that it was out in the open, Gamble showed what was probably an official sadness. 'He was a fine man and I shall never forgive myself, because I must have underesti-mated the possibility of him being exposed.'

Rogers, having swallowed much of his irritation, asked, 'Why weren't we told? This is our particular bailiwick and telling us that you're on it is the required official form.'

'Your Chief Constable was told at the time and he agreed that for the sergeant's safety it should go no further. Until the balloon went up this morning and I was passed to Mr Pitt-Bowsher, it hadn't.'

'A pity,' Rogers said, unimpressed, for that form of secrecy could point to a mistaken lack of confidence in the incorruptibility of his department. 'Had we known and co-operated, this might not have happened. Was Fowler his proper name?'

Gamble shook his head. 'No. The point I have to make is that it would suit our purpose – desperately so – that, whatever you may happen to find out, he was killed for reasons other than having been exposed as an undercover agent. I would want you to go on believing, as it were, that he is Henry Fowler, a former employee of the Haughton-le-Swale Safari Park, which he actually was ten years or so ago before he joined the service. What I'm telling you stays with you only; not to be passed to anyone else, a confidant or not.'

'I can manage that, though I'll have to know what he was undercover for.'

Gamble hesitated, clearly feeling any answer to be comparable to having nails pulled from his fingers.

Rogers, recognizing the hesitation, said coldly, 'I *am* a police officer, as you may recall. If I'm not to be trusted with whatever's going on, it's a certainty I shall let slip something that'll put the brakes on whatever you're up to.'

He eyed Gamble speculatively, ready to read the truth or the absence of it in the answer he was forcing from him. 'I could make a guess, you know,' he offered sardonically, 'and accept that it's a drugs ring you're hoping to infiltrate. Is that so?'

Gamble hadn't been adept enough to cover up from Rogers, even had he wanted to, and, grimacing at the silent Pitt-Bowsher, said, 'As you will. It's a couple of million pounds' worth of amphetamine tablet manufacturing with an active distribution branch believed to be connected with Caldbeck Castle . . .' – he showed a sudden excess of caution – '. . . and that's all I'm authorized to tell you. Now perhaps you'll put it out of your mind and deal specifically and obviously with the two killings as you've already been doing.'

Pitt-Bowsher, intervening, said, 'I'm afraid I shall have to make that an order, Mr Rogers.'

'I shall bear in mind what you've told me,' Rogers responded baldly, his irritation still not expended. 'My intention will be, as before, to concentrate on identifying, arresting and charging the person responsible and not to rupture myself over anything outside it.'

Though both Pitt-Bowsher and Gamble weren't obviously approving of his attitude, they said nothing, and that wasn't worrying Rogers. He said, 'You've not mentioned it, but I've had Fowler's room at his lodgings searched, though I'm still waiting for the result.'

'There'll be nothing of significance there; the sergeant would know what he was doing.' Gamble seemed not to think that of any importance. 'But thank you anyway.'

'And what if I do happen to pick up something that's none of my business?'

'I'll leave a number with Mr Pitt-Bowsher who'll liaise with me over whatever you have.' Changing tack, possibly to chop the disgruntled Rogers short, Gamble said, 'Don't expect an identification on Fowler's prints either. That's already been cancelled.' He grimaced. 'I was told they'd been taken from my sergeant who was then described as dead. You couldn't guess how I felt . . . virtually sending one of my men to his death.'

'Bad for him, too,' a sardonic Rogers pointed out. 'Is it going to surprise you if it's proved that he was having it off with Mrs Stoner in his own time, or even if it's connected with the enquiry you sent him on?'

Gamble wasn't going too far with that, and Pitt-Bowsher kept his distance by pulling at his bottom lip and staring out of the window on the opposite side of the room. 'He's a single man . . .' – Gamble's eyebrows were down and he looked uncomfortable – '. . . and I think he'd be prepared to put aside the morality of what he was doing in cultivating anybody who he believed might be a source of information. I don't think I'd quarrel with that.'

'At a pinch I don't suppose I would either,' Rogers agreed, 'but I thought you might. As I am not going to know who he is, I expect you'll be responsible for notifying his relatives of his death?'

'He had none. Not in this country at least, so leave it with me. For your information, I've seen his body and I've identified him.' He began shifting in his chair, buttoning his jacket over his pot belly as if ready to leave. 'I'm sure you'll act as if this meeting had never taken place. It goes almost without saying that what we've discussed is to be left behind in this office; that none of your staff is given the slightest whiff of what you've been told.'

He lifted himself from the chair, not without a strained grunt or two, as Rogers said stiffly, standing also, 'That's not likely and it's a matter about which I don't need reminding.' Gamble's being a chief superintendent didn't make him outrank Rogers who wasn't prepared to take any stick from a man who appeared to believe that drugs trafficking was more important than murder.

'I have every confidence that you don't,' Gamble assured him, unmoved and apparently willing to humour a justifiably annoyed Rogers, already having written finish to his version of the Law of the Medes and Persians. 'In the meantime we'll have to assume that our man Fowler hasn't been twigged; that we can carry on in that belief. At least until I decide on what our next move is to be; so the less you know about what's happening on the other side of the fence, the better it is.'

'One thing then before I go,' Rogers put to him, giving him a direct stare. 'You can minimize my possible tripping over something or other by clearing, or not clearing, Mrs Wing. She's the head of security at the park and I have to work closely with her, keep her full confidence if I'm to get anywhere.'

He had the answer he more or less expected, which was no answer at all from Gamble's wholly unrevealing features. Instead, he held out a fat bone-squeezing hand to be shaken and said formally, 'It's been a pleasure, Mr Rogers. We shall keep in touch.'

'A minute,' Rogers said, certain that he was being hurried

off. 'If you can't tell me about Mrs Wing, you can about whoever it is in the executive hierarchy who's organizing this set-up for you. There *is* someone, isn't there?'

Gamble looked angry for a moment, then agreed, 'Yes, there is.'

'Shouldn't I know who?'

'We don't think so.'

'You can trust him?' There was a sort of unspoken 'More than you can me?' in his words.

'Completely. His brother's a highly regarded civil servant in one of the Military Intelligence departments.' He added reprovingly, 'We do know what we're doing, Mr Rogers,' with the detective verging on pointing out that having had a planted undercover agent murdered didn't quite seem like it.

Out from the office with the fence-sitting Pitt-Bowsher having nodded his dismissal and losing no time in stuffing his neglected pipe with as much tobacco as it could hold, Rogers had to admit that he would probably have acted in precisely the same information-grudging way as had Gamble.

Opening the doors of his car to allow its contained baking heat to dissipate into more hot air and waiting, he knew that, intended or not, Gamble had left him with a half-formed suspicion that there could be either a leak from his squad or – taking it to extremes – a possible informer in Rogers's own department.

He thought it significant that nothing had been said by Gamble about the possibility of the murderer – assuming the killings to be drug-related – having decided on a run for it. Or, for that matter, about whether the dead Fowler had a contact remaining in the park.

That, as he climbed into his slow-cooling car, left him with the too-delectable-for-his-peace-of-mind Lesley Wing to worry about; to wonder whether there was need to be careful in his future dealing with her. Something about her fortuitous introduction to the subject of the summerhouse now began to erode his confidence in her as an aide and he cursed the probable unwisdom of the question he had put to Gamble about her.

# 13

Rogers, seated in the Murder Wagon, squeezed into his almost spaceless office cubicle, was feeling a mite glum over the
police canteen's version of the two toasted cheese and tomato
sandwiches he had eaten in a hurry and which seemed to be
hanging half-way down his oesophagus, their passage eased
only fractionally by the accompaniment of a glass of un-
chilled Liebfraumilch. Too, while at Headquarters and having
checked to see if there were any telephone calls logged for his
attention – there had been, depressingly, nothing from Angharad – he had then twice called her number without reply.
Now, with the reputedly dangerous body of Woman Sergeant
Flowers standing necessarily cheek by jowl with him while
she reported on what she had collated in his absence, he was
made conscious of her intimidating uniformed breasts radiat-
ing unneeded warmth and the fragrance of eau-de-Cologne a
bare couple of hands' reach from his nose.

Flowers, sniffing pointedly about something she was sens-
ing in his attitude, told him that Dr Twite had committed
himself to a four o'clock examination of the bodies of Harriet
Stoner and Henry Fowler. He had added – she thought wittily
– that he would be delighted to be assured that Superintendent Rogers's own body and pathological virtuosity would be
in attendance.

There had been telephone calls for him from Mrs Wing and
from Mr Latouche the veterinary whom she hadn't met, but
sounded as if she would like to. He, she said, seemed worried
and quite agitated at Rogers's absence, asking for a call from
him on his return.

Inspector Hassell had reported verbally that the shotgun
believed to have been used in the murder had not so far been
found, but he was continuing the search and augmenting it by
calling out the subaqua team to search the stream adjacent to

the summerhouse. That, Rogers thought, was a bloody nuisance, for it might mean that the shotgun was being kept for a future murderous use; for whom, who could know?

Finally, Flowers said that Chief Inspector Lingard had reported in to speak to him and, in his continued absence, had himself gone to the park restaurant to see if they served a decent meal and – she also thought that was meant humorously – he would hold Superintendent Rogers personally responsible should he suffer ptomaine poisoning or anything like it.

'Have him turfed out, will you, sergeant,' he asked her, 'and he's to be back here at his fastest. I want to be out of here as soon as I can.'

When the highly efficient Flowers had taken herself and her awe-inspiring bosom the five or so yards back to her own office – Rogers was left remembering that such breasts were said to be a certain, off-putting and dangerous indication of a fruitful fertility – he had to contemplate the reading of the thin sheaf of reports she had left with him.

Before settling down to those, he telephoned Lesley Wing – he had liked it that she had sounded so pleased to hear from him – telling her that he was manifestly back in being and would she help him by organizing Quentin Coope to be available in her office in about – he looked at his watch – thirty minutes, but prepared, if necessary, to hang on for a further fluid ten minutes or so.

Then he spoke to Latouche who was in his surgery and who said that he was sorry, but he was about to begin some relatively minor surgery on a lioness's leg and could Rogers ring again later in the afternoon. He said – sounding only a little concerned – that he would like a further talk with Rogers, chiefly about their previous conversation, about which there was no great hurry.

Replacing the receiver, he thought that it could only be words about Harriet Stoner that Latouche wanted, and his earlier suspicion hardened that there had been a leg-over situation between the two of them.

His local Identification Bureau report which he had started

to read told him that preliminary name checks on Wimbush, Bloor, Latouche, Coope and Halcro had been made with nothing known against any of them. This, Rogers knew, didn't amount to anything much and left him assured of nothing.

A National Identification Bureau check on the fingerprints of Harriet Stoner née Gager revealed that two and a half years previously she had been convicted at Kingsbridgeton Crown Court of conspiracy to defraud in the name of Harriet Louise Gager and sentenced to six months' imprisonment, suspended.

A similar check on William Albert Stoner revealed an eleven-year-old conviction at a Plymouth Naval Court Martial convened on HMS *Totnes,* a shore establishment, when he was sentenced to six months' imprisonment in a naval detention establishment with a reduction of his rank to that of Marine and dismissed the service on his release for indecent assaults on a Wren then serving on board the same ship.

There had been no return on the fingerprints of Henry Fowler, the IB assuring Rogers that they were chasing up NIB about this omission. 'And good luck to you,' Rogers grunted to the distant and unhearing IB.

Finally – 'Thank God,' he muttered to himself – there was a belated report from DS Johnson to the effect that he and WPC Farrar had searched Fowler's rented room at Wrag Barn Cottage and had recovered a few personal documents, some books and a loaded camera. These had been placed under sealed cover for Rogers's information. He, in turn, thought that he might as well garner what he could from the documents and then send them, the books and the camera on to Pitt-Bowsher, the ACC, for forwarding to Gamble. Poor Fowler would have been lacking in initiative had he not taken the opportunity of photographing any *dramatis personae* of interest to the Crime Squad.

When he refilled his still-hot pipe and lit it almost absently, still being able to see the ceiling through the haze of smoke, he knew that having weighed it all up, he wasn't a hell of a lot nearer knowing any more than he'd known before leaving Lesley and the promise of a decent lunch.

Which reminded him. Though it made him feel a five-star bastard, he called out to Flowers to give him a call to Headquarters. When she had, he spoke to the IB, lowering his voice and asking for a check on Lesley Wing's army career and general background, including anything findable about her husband, the result to be passed to him under sealed cover. Impartiality, he thought wryly, was supposed to be the All; even when applied to a woman whom the basement of his mind insisted on visualizing as looking up at him, black-haired and pale-bodied against the imagined background of a turquoise blue sheet and pillows.

He was brooding on this desirable tableau, seemingly with no impetus to get moving on anything – he thought it might be the oppressive heat held captive in the thinly walled coach – when he heard the deep rumbling of Lingard's Bentley approaching.

Jaunty and nonchalant, looking freshly shaved and scrubbed and immaculate in his white suit, he belied any suggestion that the afternoon's heat had had any adverse effect on him. It was the kind of attitude that blond hair, blue eyes and a superfluity of money seemed to naturally acquire. Unable to share comfortably Rogers's telephone kiosk of an office, he leaned elegantly in the doorway.

'I hear that His Eminence the dreaded ACC has finally caught up with you while I've been seeing the horrors and excesses of incarceration in our prisons,' he said, tapping a fingernail on his ivory snuff box to loosen any grains caught up on the lid. 'You need an alibi or similar?'

'It was nothing,' Rogers told him offhandedly. 'Being a double murder, he wanted to know the ins and outs of it for his next conference with the Chief Constable.' He put on an expression of disgust. 'All in all, a load of balls. Before you start, let me brief you on our progress, or our signal lack of it.' He did it without once actually mentioning Lesley Wing by name, which should have rung a bell of sorts with the astute Lingard.

When he had finished, he asked, 'Have you done the check on Mrs Stoner's room yet?'

Lingard grimaced. 'No time yet, George. It'll be done when I've written up on Laurence Stoner and tied up with Mrs Wing.'

'I think we should do it sooner rather than later. Stoner might have reasons for doing a search of her stuff himself.' He shrugged away his momentary concern. 'So, how did you get on at Crouch Aughton?'

Lingard gave him a quick grin, apparently having recognized an evasion of sorts when he had had one tossed to him, and inhaled a generous fix of his snuff. 'I met a Detective Inspector Whincut whom we might try and persuade to apply for a transfer to our force, specifically to our department. When I've taken over your cooling chair, George, I shall certainly do it if you don't. Everything's right about him except his taste in coffee. He put me on to Laurence Stoner for a starter – he's a stepbrother of our apparently detestable William Albert – who's a cold-blooded uncaring bastard in his own right if I've ever met one.'

'My chair won't be cooling just yet, David,' Rogers said easily. Lingard, his friend as well as his second-in-command, was the almost certain future successor to his office, and that partly on his own unqualified recommendation. 'Fill me in on Stoner and forget for the moment your plans to unseat me.'

Lingard smiled and said, 'Egad, George, you didn't do me any favour in sending me to look for him. He's in the Harden-huish Open Prison, *soi disant*, and I doubt the nastiest of Queen's Counsels could get anything truthful from him.' Then he gave Rogers, a man impatient of verbal windiness, a laconic account of his interview with Laurence Stoner; a man, he said, carrying around with him a load of grief for someone.

'You'll see', he continued, intending to amplify some of his remarks to his apparently unimpressed senior, 'that he has some sort of connection with the park. Tenuous, 'tis true, but probably strengthened because I didn't have to jump on his face to get it. He actually said the village, but it's the same thing in yardage, isn't it?'

'Having parked his mistreated girlfriend – I think we'll go on calling her Mrs Harriet Stoner until we're sure – with his stepbrother for whatever reason other than the one he gives, I'd say yes, it is.' Rogers was speaking around the stem of the pipe he was relighting.

'I've a feeling he was exaggerating Harriet's promiscuities, bless her wherever she is,' Lingard murmured. 'You think?'

'Could be,' Rogers partly agreed. 'How many different and accommodating males does it take? And how often? And I don't expect an answer to that.' He was silent for a few moments while he listened to Flowers indistinctly answering her telephone in her office. 'I'm certainly not happy about the reason for his dumping her on his wretched stepbrother.'

'Who would be?' Lingard echoed him derisively. 'To put her improbably out of the reach of his friends' indecencies?'

'More understandably, I'd guess, to put her somewhere where pressures couldn't be put on her to talk about him and his dodgy activities while he's in prison.' Rogers couldn't tell Lingard what pressures he was referring to in theory, but he was reasonably confident it wasn't to keep her sexually quarantined from any lecherous friends he might have. 'Incidentally, was your friend Whincut exaggerating about the open prison?'

'If he was,' Lingard said, 'it wasn't by much.'

'If Stoner *is* primarily concerned in this business of ours, then he has to have a connection with one of the keepers to get access to the shotgun.' He grimaced and shook his head. 'I might be bloody stupid, but check it out, will you?'

'I think we have to,' Lingard agreed, 'though I'm prepared to believe almost anything about the cunning bugger, but what he says himself.'

'Good.' Rogers had finished and was about to get out from his inadequately stuffed and confining chair which was doing little for the comfort of his buttocks. 'I have to leave now. Do me a favour, David. I've overlooked something, so when you're doing your thing about Stoner's possible connection with a bent keeper and possibly seeing Halcro the head keeper, have a look at the gun cupboard. Give me your opinion on its security and whether his complaint of theft stands up to examination. If he's agreeable, borrow one of the guns he has left and some of each of the two types of cartridges he holds. And ask him not to mention the borrowing to anybody. When you've done that, see if you can confirm or not our Stoner's loss of his testicles. I might then be able to have some civilized sympathy – some, not too much – for the nasty little sod. And if it comes down to a question of horses for courses, I'm still putting my money on his being the one we'll be charging at the end of the day.'

It left him with the verging on disquieting thought that it wasn't unknown to both him and Lingard that prisoners had been discovered operating – even in so-called high security units – within drugs cartels with arrogant ease while inside. Stoner would have been given even more opportunities in an open prison, and Rogers's inability to discuss it with his second-in-command in particular was wormwood and gall to him.

And when Lingard heard of it – as eventually he would – his understandable anger would be caustic and uninhibited, probably leaving his senior with a wish to drop everything and emigrate to the far reaches of Australia.

## 14

Rogers, an unwilling occupant of a desk chair and his car seat too often for his well-being, chose to walk the thousand or so yards to Lesley Wing's office, finding the road and footpaths thronged with early afternoon visitors. He interrupted his walk to stand, but for a deep ditch and green-meshed fencing, almost face to face with a magnificant Siberian tiger.

She – he accepted her to be a tigress – stood confronting him, huge and impossibly beautiful in her whitish yellow and bistre-striped coat, her amber eyes in her huge cat's face look-ing sadly, almost appealingly, at him. More beautiful, he thought recklessly, than any living human being.

He accepted that he could be getting the wrong message

from her, not overlooking that she was capable when necessary of a chilling ferocity, but the brief contact – it had been
disturbingly palpable – left him feeling sad, not only for her
and her kind, but for all the cats of the world, living and dying
largely at the whim and usually selfish needs of his own
species. In Rogers's own opinion and experience, man was the
most savage and merciless predator of them all.

A shirt-sleeved Lesley, friendly but not overly so, was alone
in her well-foliaged office with no sign of Coope waiting on
Rogers's arrival. He had, she told Rogers wryly, looking at her
office clock, made it clear that he would be unable to attend
until three o'clock, fifteen minutes away.

'Not only that,' she said, indicating the visitors' chair at the
side of her desk for him to be seated, 'but Stoner has telephoned in to say that he was taking this afternoon off in
order to contact his family about Harriet's death. He said he
would be back for his six o'clock shift. I imagine you'd like to
see him then?'

Rogers wasn't in too much of a hurry about that. Stoner
would have to come into his reckoning at some time, prefer-
ably when he knew more about him than he did now. More to
the point, he was feeling constrained in his association with a
woman he couldn't believe to be a party to a drugs syndicate
or whatever it was; constrained to show a false front to her in
case she actually was. He said, 'Yes, I would. Neither he nor
anyone else is yet in the clear.' Not Stoner for certain, for he
was lodged in his mind as a primary suspect. Not that he had
the shadow of evidence pointing to him, but his policeman's
sixth sense was telling him that the offensive bastard *could*
have had a motive.

'When you do see him, use my office by all means.'

'I'd be grateful. I'm sorry about the lunch.' Rogers had the
impression that she had cooled a little in her regard of him, a
possible reflection of his own always difficult to conceal feelings. 'Because we've a double death here, the ACC needed
some special briefing.' He forced a smile. 'Missed lunches are
all part of the job. Keep me in mind, will you?'

She had smiled back at him, a possible confirmation, if he

could believe it, that he was still *persona grata*.'If you're still here later on, perhaps some tea?'

'I'll look forward,' he promised, 'though I've a necessary attendance in the Abbotsburn mortuary yet to come. Which reminds me. Could you be available at your Point B gate at ten forty-five tonight?'

'With you?' Seeing confirmation in his nod, she said, 'I'll be there. Are you going to tell me why?'

'It's necessary hush-hush stuff which you'll know about only when the time comes.' He had said that, he thought, pretty lamely. 'You don't mind?'

She said, 'No,' though she sounded doubtful. 'You know Stoner will be making his eleven o'clock point there tonight? Does that affect what you'll be there for?'

'It certainly would.' He was frowning, his eyebrows down. 'Would it be possible to change his time there?'

'Only if you didn't mind him demanding a reason which I wouldn't have. I could give him time off, of course – insist on it because of Harriet's death – and put on Kate Docherty in his place.'

'She's on your establishment?' He was momentarily surprised.

'Why on earth not? You think she'd do better if she wore trousers?'

Bloody hell, I've walked right into it, he told himself, recognizing female asperity when it was directed at him. 'I'm sorry,' he apologized. 'That wasn't my intention at all. Perhaps we'd better let it be, for I might want to speak to him afterwards.' Hearing the sound of somebody entering the outside parade room, he said, 'I think I hear Coope.'

'Use my desk,' she invited him, reaching for her twill jacket draped on the back of her chair. 'I shall see you later when you're back.'

He was at the door, holding the handle and ready to open it for her. She stood her ground, her jacket half on, her expression suddenly puzzled. 'There's something wrong, isn't there, George?' she said as if unsure of herself. 'Tell me what I've done.'

Bloody hell again, he thought unhappily, seeing an end to the affection developing between them, and damn this unfair feminine intuition thing. Aloud and almost brusquely, he said, 'I don't understand what you mean, Lesley. If there's anything wrong it's with me, not you. It's this bloody-minded ACC I've got on my back, and who's digging his spurs in.' This fictional excuse was a minor humiliation for him to suffer; minor, but hurting to his pride.

'I hope so,' she replied, seemingly unconvinced and without her usual brightness, passing him in a waft of scent and through the door he was holding open for her.

Trying to put pleasantness in his words, he forced a smile at the tall youth waiting in the parade office who had apparently been pacing up and down during the past minute or so. 'Mr Coope,' he said. 'I'm sorry if I've kept you waiting. Come in and take a seat.'

Rogers, seated at the desk in Lesley's chair – it was still warm and impressed from her body's use of it – did his policeman's careful assessment of Coope's externals, being convinced that a man's lying would almost always show itself in an interrogation, no matter how superficially friendly it might seem to be.

He was unmistakably that year's university fodder with his fan of youthful springy straw-coloured hair, worn with a centre parting which allowed a wing of it to fall each side of the steel-rimmed granny glasses and framing a small-nosed pink-mouthed face. Oddly good-looking enough, Rogers supposed – and topping some six feet of muscular body – to bring on a few hot flushes in a not-too-discerning teenaged girl's inexperienced bosom. He was now showing what could only be a cocky air of self-conceit, and this apparently fascinating one-time lover of an older Harriet Stoner came packaged in the current male fashion of sagging fabric, tailored – only God could possibly know why – into baggy unsightly clothing, putting Rogers's admittedly conventional teeth on edge even before he had started. Still, and for all that, he thought sardonically, Coope probably knew what made things like zip fasteners work and could explain more or less intelligently

103

how Doppler's principle could be applied to the theory of an expanding universe.

'I won't keep you too long,' Rogers started. 'I take it you've already heard of the deaths of Mrs Stoner and Henry Fowler?'

'Yes.' That had seemed a wary enough response.

'A sad happening,' Rogers commented, no admirer of taciturnity in potential informants and keeping his eye-to-eye contact.

'I think so.' He raised what sounded to be a good-accented voice into something resembling arrogance. 'Is that why I'm here?'

'It is. You knew Mrs Stoner in particular, I understand?'

Coope jerked his head in apparent surprise. 'I did? I'm sorry, but if you've been told that then you've been misinformed.'

'A pity,' Rogers said mildly. 'You might have been of some help in finding out who killed her so brutally. And your working colleague Fowler also, of course.' He believed, and hoped, that the canteen's sandwiches had finally found lodgement in his stomach, feeling more disposed to an amiability even with somebody so patently dodging the issue.

Coope overdid the shrugging of his shoulders, his dark blue eyes behind the granny glasses looking at a point above Rogers's head. 'If you think so, though I doubt it.'

Rogers's voice was now tersely official and he was unsmiling. 'The two witnesses who've approached me about Mrs Stoner's male associates – people in some authority, I should add – have both said quite specifically that you and she were often seen together in circumstances which suggested you were – to put it at its best – sexually intimate. Certainly Mrs Stoner appears not to have made any secret of it.' He had been holding Coope's sometimes wavering attention by his hard unblinking stare, and he had noted the convulsive spasm in his throat at his last words.

'My ... My father is the vicar in charge of the parishes of Croker-sub-Castle,' he said with a visible unease, 'and I'm certainly unlikely to be sexually intimate, as you've put it, with any married woman. Indeed,' he added in a sudden show of high-flown indignation, 'no more than my father ever would with any woman not his wife.'

'I'm talking about you, not your father.' Rogers now knew that Coope was on the defensive, and that was most usually the cover for something to hide. 'I'd prefer that you didn't bring him into this interview unless you've no objection to the Croker-sub-Castle police making a few local enquiries to substantiate or otherwise what you're telling me. This is a matter of murder and my own enquiries sometimes need to be far-reaching. Think about it,' he emphasized sternly. 'And *now.*'

The silence in the stifling office was heavy with hard thinking, the detective hearing in it the agitated breathing of Coope and seeing the tremor of his fingers which he was trying to still against his thighs. He felt sorry for the youth, yet intent on forcing the truth from him.

Impatient at his waiting and concerned about the approaching time of Twite's examination of the two bodies, he said gently, reasonably, 'There would be nothing unlawful or socially objectionable in your making love to Mrs Stoner were that all and, so far as that is concerned, nothing of it need go outside the knowledge of myself and whatever officially secret records we keep in my department.'

He tapped cold ash from his pipe into Lesley's metal desk bin, leaving a few moments for Coope to reflect or not on the morality of having been seduced – as Rogers thought he must have been – by an older and more sexually experienced woman.

When there was no clear sign of a forthcoming admission, Rogers said, 'Most of us – and I include myself – go through that phase in our growing up, and I've little doubt that you can say much the same of your own experience with other students from whichever school or college you attended. So?' he invited him with a fairly amiable expression in his face. 'May we have a meeting of minds over a woman so brutally done to death?'

'Shouldn't I be told who it was that said they saw me with Mrs Stoner?'

Rogers shook his head. 'No, you shouldn't. You are expecting my discretion; they equally expect it for them. Dammit,' he pointed out to him, 'I'm not about to bite your head off because you had a bit on the side while you were away from home, am I?'

'No, I suppose not,' Coope muttered glumly. Then, as if he had experienced a sudden resurgence of confidence, 'It was no big deal anyway. I hadn't been here more than a few days before she asked me to sleep with her. She's older than I am – quite a lot, I think – and attractive enough, though a bit flashy.' He grimaced, as Rogers felt he damned well should after that denigration of a dead woman who had been his lover. 'I'd left my girlfriend behind in Croker and I was in no mood to be too monastic about someone like Mrs Stoner and what she needed from me.' He paused, then said, 'Is that what you wanted?'

Detaching his gaze from the youth, Rogers started to fill his pipe, lighting it and blowing smoke to the ceiling. Life would now feel a lot more acceptable. 'I'm sure there's more,' he pressed him amiably, 'and I've no doubt that a confession of a sort is always good for the soul.'

'I don't care that much, and I never have,' Coope said, not responding to amiability and now clearly regarding Rogers as if he were a stuffed shirt representative of a contemporary Spanish Inquisition.

'We don't afterwards, do we? It's in the nature of the beast. Where did all this happen? In your bed? Her bed? In a hedge?'

When Coope hesitated, the beginnings of an angry scowl on his face, Rogers put the boot in, barking out at him, 'For God's sake, man, stop acting like a bloody third-form schoolboy or we'll be here all afternoon.'

Coope kept his scowl, but spoke. 'It was a guest house in Thurnholme Bay. I've forgotten the name of it if I ever remembered. After that, here in the park, but never in her house.'

'In the back garden of her lodgings? In the alligator's pool?' Rogers was at his most saturnine.

Coope looked at him as if he were mad. 'You want to know where?'

'It'd help.' Rogers was already figuring on its being the summerhouse of tragic assignation.

'The old summerhouse,' he forced out from behind his teeth, visibly hating the detective. 'It was her choice ... it gave me the creeps. I'm not easily embarrassed, but I didn't want to live too long with the feeling that somebody was going to barge in and cause trouble.'

'Such as her brother-in-law?' Rogers was sweating, wondering why Coope had apparently been born without pores.

He looked surprised. 'Why would he? She was nothing to do with him in that respect. She was lodging there, coming and going as she pleased.'

'But she held in her the potential embarrassment of being a married woman, of course.'

'That's true. I'm sorry I said that about her. I suppose everybody here knew about it?'

'Perhaps. And no doubt that included her husband.'

'I do doubt it. He'd left her for another woman and she talked about him with complete dislike.'

'I've been told that she was frightened of him.'

Not having yet been struck dead for his sins, Coope was getting back the cockiness he had come in with. 'Not so. At least, not how she told me. She was scared, it's true; but of somebody working here in the park, not her husband.'

'There's a name?'

He shook his head, his hair flopping over his forehead until pushed back with his hand. 'Not remotely. Nor was I particularly interested.' He snickered. 'She asked me to take her away – God knows where to, though she did suggest Ireland ...' – his voice rose in incredulity – '... but I wasn't having any of that, was I, and I said so. How could I? I pointed out to her that I was waiting for my university placing and I'd no intention of taking her or anybody else anywhere. That's when I called it a day on what we were doing.'

'I don't imagine it was all that easy.' Rogers guessed that Coope had been lacking large amounts of finesse in detaching himself from the luckless Harriet. Even if he had taken the initiative, which he manifestly hadn't.

'It wasn't so bad either. We had an argument and she cried a bit and all that. I think she must have put most of it on because I saw her a few evenings later going out of the park with one of the security guards.'

'And he was?' Bloor, he guessed: almost certainly.

'I don't know.' He was a poor liar, but not one to press at the moment. 'I only saw the back of him.'

'Well, that settles that then,' Rogers said cheerfully in an obviously relaxed mood. 'Fairly painless, yes?'

'Does that mean you won't take it further? To where my parents may hear of it?'

'Not unless. Of course not,' Rogers assured him rather ambiguously. Relighting the tobacco in his gone-out pipe and speaking around its stem, he said, seemingly mildly interested, 'I understand you're a collector of moths or something similar.'

'I propose reading for a degree in one of the biological sciences and entomology specifically. I'm using my gap year in studying the *Noctuidae*, not collecting them. That's quite a different thing.'

'I take it that these are night-flying moths, needing you to do your studying them after dark. Yes?' He was feeling as if he were in the hot steam of a sauna bath, his shoes seemingly full of moist sand, his underclothing sticking to his body like flock wallpaper.

'Yes, though I'd like to repeat that I'm not a collector in the sense that I kill them and stick pins in them. I don't care for that, and I shall be breeding them one day under controlled conditions. For study, of course. You want me to go on?' He appeared to have stopped hating Rogers.

'I'd like to be told what you do here at night.'

'What I said. My present interest is in the eggs, larvae, pupae and in particular in the imagos – the sexually mature insects. Oh, and naturally the food plants they subsist on.' The light of the true enthusiast was in his eyes. 'You've heard of the Setaceous Hebrew Character? The Square-spot Rustic? They're actually breeding here now and ...'

Rogers shut off his sudden volubility by holding up his open hand. 'Please,' he said. 'It sounds most interesting, but I haven't the time. I'm more concerned in your method of studying them. I'm told you've been given a free hand to go round the park at night to do it?'

'Mr Wimbush was good enough to allow me, yes.' He had suddenly withdrawn his enthusiasm.

'Tell me what you do and where you do it. I recall – possibly faultily – that collectors anyway used sugar or treacle to lure what I must say are unfortunate moths on to chosen trunks of trees.' Rogers had no time for those who shed the yellow blood of moths or butterflies. Coope, whatever his reasons, earned his approval for not doing so; Harriet Stoner being another matter altogether.

In watching Coope while he talked, and trying to see him through the eyes of a hungry husbandless woman, a surmise that Lesley just might have been attracted to him crept unwanted into his thinking; being almost immediately pushed back into the basement of his mind from where, unwanted, it had come.

'It's still used – I do sugar the occasional tree – but the street lights here, being mercury-vapour lamps, are better. I can reach the moths that are attracted to them easily with the portable ladder I sometimes bring with me.'

'The lights are distributed throughout the park?'

'Yes, though there aren't many. Most are switched off at midnight from the security office.'

'And you're about with your net until then?'

'I go out regularly from after supper – that's about ten thirty – until I've had enough; usually about half-past eleven because I still have my notes to write up.'

'You carry your own light, do you?'

'Of course. I use a shielded flashlight.'

'You're very visible then?'

'I am. There's no reason why I shouldn't be.'

'Do you make a nightly visit to any street light or tree somewhat adjacent to the summerhouse, with which you're already well familiar?' Rogers was pressing him now and knowing that it would soon have its effect on Coope's composure.

'A tree, but not all that near.'

'So how near?' Rogers had noticed a marked wariness in his attitude.

'About ten to fifteen yards.' There had been an only just perceptible hesitation in saying that.

'What time was your visit?'

'Very approximately at half-past ten. It would be one of the nearest to my lodgings.'

'Could you see that it was occupied from where you were?'

'When I was passing in the lane I saw that it was, but only because I could see Mr Fowler's car parked inside the gate.' There was a sheen of sweat glistening on his forehead and he was manifestly unhappy.

'The car was unoccupied?'

'Yes. I did shine my flashlight on it. That's how I knew it was his car.'

'Why would he go there in his car when he only lodges a short distance away?'

'I don't know, but probably because he'd have gone out in it with her earlier in the evening.'

'You've a car, I imagine?'

'Yes. An Austin Mini.'

'Is that what you did with Mrs Stoner? Go out in your car, then park it outside the summerhouse on your return?'

'Two or three times, yes. There's less chance of somebody walking in on you if they see a car there.' He hesitated. 'Is that where they were killed? Were they there then?'

'Probably yes to your first question; I don't know to your second.' Coope was looking rather sick and Rogers pushed on. 'While you were there, or near there, did you hear a gunshot?'

'A gunshot?' he echoed blankly. 'You mean in the summerhouse?'

'Not necessarily. Just a gunshot. Anywhere.'

'I didn't hear one at all. Not after I'd left my lodgings. And certainly not before, because I couldn't from there.'

Rogers stared hard at him. 'It *was* heard by other people outside the park. You're sure?'

'I'm sure *I* didn't.'

Rogers shrugged, suggesting a degree of disbelief. 'Before you returned, who had you seen moving around the park? Somebody who had probably also seen you?'

Coope banged his forehead rather dramatically with the heel of his hand. 'That's difficult, for though anyone may have passed behind me, I might not have bothered to see who it was. Certainly I saw Mr Halcro, and once Mr Stoner, the security guard, in his golf cart.'

'Where were you then?'

'I honestly don't remember,' Coope said helplessly. 'Probably somewhere in the middle; it's impossible for me to say.'

'Are you quite certain you didn't see anyone when you were near the summerhouse?'

When there was no reply from the youth, his face showing strain and indecision, Rogers said, 'Dammit, laddie; I know you did. You're inviting serious trouble to hit you. Who did you see?'

'I don't know . . . someone in the trees.'

'Near the summerhouse, of course?'

'A shadow, that's all. I . . . I could have been mistaken.'

'No, you couldn't. You're just scared.' He scowled at him. 'You realize, don't you, that whoever it was could see you and recognize you?'

Coope shook his head. 'A shadow. That was all.'

'But you didn't hear a gunshot at about half-past ten?'

'No. I said not.'

Rogers stared hard at him, seeking the truth or not from behind the granny glasses. 'I need you to be sure about what you've told me,' he told him sternly. 'It's important that you've told me the truth and nothing less than it.'

'I'm sure I have,' Coope said unhappily. He was silent for long moments until, with his face set in a determined expression, he said, 'Will you tell me why my going out with Mrs Stoner a month ago should bother you so much?'

'It doesn't brother me,' Rogers told him with full gravitas. 'Not at the moment it doesn't, but it might.' Then, unsticking himself from his chair with a not very reassuring change of face at what he now thought to be an anxiously sweating Coope, he said, 'However, I make the point that if you *are* withholding from me anything significant about your association with Mrs Stoner or, indeed, anyone else then you must hope that a retributive nemesis isn't waiting for you around the next corner.'

Out in the sunshine – which wasn't going to do his half-baked body much good either – he was conscious that Harriet Stoner and Henry Fowler were by now being decanted by a no doubt increasingly irritated Wilfred Twite, a man inclined to an after-lunch tetchiness at any late arrival at what could, in his opinion, be his pathological *chef-d'oeuvre*.

# 15

If there was anything remotely pleasant about being not yet dead in a mortuary, a still heated-up Rogers considered it might be that it contained in itself a welcome coolness.

It was well after half-past four and he had been dodging around among trammelled wildlife for twelve hours. After a bare three hours' sleep the previous night it was beginning to tell. Only beginning, though it was becoming inclined to take its toll in clear thinking and aching legs.

In this formalin-smelling theatre of the unspeakably grue-some, there were two side-by-side stainless steel necropsy tables, each carrying face-upwards a brilliantly illuminated bloodstained and pallid-fleshed body on which an overhead black hose dribbled water.

Twite, dressed fatly in his surgeon's green gown and red rubber apron, was not nearly so tetchy on Rogers's late arrival as he had expected. This could mean only that he had had a satisfying lunch paid for by someone else or that his love life was firing on all cylinders and not interfering with his interest in stripping bloodily the now quite seriously dead Henry

Fowler's skull of his scalp. The scented smoke from the cigarette he held between his lips was a welcome, if not quite strong enough, fumigant against the terrible smell of blood and raw flesh.

It had been one of Rogers's longest held incomprehensibilities how otherwise civilized and fastidious pathologists – especially Twite the gourmet and lover of women in particular – could ignore or suppress human nature's disgust and repulsion against cutting into and mutilating the human body; and, in so doing, to be seemingly unaware of the often sickening stench of putrefaction of the decomposing flesh left behind at death.

Behind Twite, a khaki-overalled delicately featured female attendant stood at the other table sewing together with ungloved hands the dreadful median scalpel cut running from the dead Harriet Stoner's throat to her belly with large white thread stitches. She might, he guessed, make love to some man later that evening with those same hands, and the inner visual image that resulted was a disturbing one. For she who had been Harriet, nothing of what had been done to her by her murderer and by Twite could disguise the splendidness of the body from which she had so manifestly gone.

With a virtual certainty about the causes of the two deaths, there was nothing that Rogers could do other than to wait on what Twite was going to tell him from his pathological dissectioning. Resting his buttocks – even they felt tired – against a clinically white working top and keeping his pipe alight, blowing out his own aromatic smoke, he disengaged his attention from the bodies, reflecting on his meeting violent death so often and in so many horrific ways and having an understandable wish to avoid it happening to himself; believing in a wishful thinking sort of way that he had a built-in impregnability to it. He was interested in it, though with the proviso that it was happening to somebody else.

Seeking temporary diversion from death's grimness by looking anywhere but in Twite's direction, he switched his thinking to the elegant and engaging Angharad Rhys Pritchard, naval officer's widow, barrister-at-law, yachtswoman and apparently now moving to be the ex-lover of a wifeless and rather hung-up detective superintendent presently engaged in supporting financially a divorced wife and her hairy and allegedly sexually impressive rugby player and live-in lover.

Unusually for Rogers, and despite Angharad's forewarning that they should each avoid walking on the other's shadow, he had formed a deep affection for her and wished to do just that. In between exercising the worries and concerns of his job, in and out of bed, he had pondered a thought or two about the possibility of their marrying, even though it would be an ironical twist to his fortunes to be married into a profession which, on the criminal side, he neither respected nor trusted.

Twite interrupted his generally morose train of thought by addressing him directly while doing something unpleasant to the side of poor Fowler's stripped skull, saying, 'The lady, George. I can confirm that the lacerations I've examined show that she was battered from above with a largish whatever it was which positively had a hard edge to it; enough to crush and distort the underlying bone, tissue and the occipital lobe of the brain. The instrument could be – almost certainly is – the butt-end of the shotgun also used against this male body I'm now working on. It would fit in with her being killed while lying on the *chaise-longue* thing in the summerhouse you mentioned. It satisfies you?'

'It's what I anticipated you'd say,' Rogers told him. 'You've a more precise time of death?'

Twite shook his head, scattering cigarette ash on Fowler's body. 'Not yet. No more than when I gave it to you before – between six and eight hours prior to my first seeing him. What did you make that?'

'Loosely, some time between ten and twelve. It probably fits,' Rogers said, 'though if you can narrow it down in the laboratory it'd help – I think.'

'I'll give it to you in my report if I can.' Twite had clearly given Rogers his present lot concerning Harriet Stoner and was now concentrating his attention of Fowler's massive head injury.

Rogers, sucking at his pipe more rapidly than he usually did – he was a leisurely smoker by habit – with the prospect of burning his tongue, put emerging thoughts of the engaging Angharad to one side, worrying himself about the equally engaging Lesley Wing.

In the simple terms in which he could best define his attitude towards her, his often impulsive lower half was bent on surrendering to her in a caught-on-the-rebound inopportune attraction, while his somewhat pi upper half sat in judgement on the pros and cons of her possible – he thought improbable – involvement in the drugs cartel.

Gamble's warning and his unhelpful refusal to clear her for his, Rogers's, guidance were acting as a prohibition against any approach to her other than a formally official one, his sense of duty warring grittily with his need – bloody stupid and selfish, his mind was telling him – to have something reassuring about her to set against what he believed to be the prospect of Angharad's desertion of him for that bloody interfering judge. When Twite again broke into his musing with something about Fowler's head injury he was perversely grateful for it.

'. . . little that I hadn't decided before,' he heard Twite saying, he not having apparently noticed Roger's inattention. 'He was almost certainly shot from above with the muzzle of the gun in virtual contact with the right squamous portion of the temporal bone, part of the charge exiting through the aperture between that and the left jawbone, rather messily destroying the cerebellum and part of the occipital lobe. Due to both the shot and the expanding gases, we have excessive mutilation of the remaining brain matter, distortion of the skull itself and gross damage to the left jaw structure.'

Ripping off his rubber gloves in small clouds of talc, he dropped them on the table to signify that he had finished, then continued, 'The pellets I've hooked out for you appear to be very much smaller than the standard size. You knew?'

'I think they're what is called dust shot, but obviously still

115

lethal when used in close contact with human skulls.' Rogers had never doubted it. 'The exit wound explains why I found pellets embedded in the wall behind the *chaise-longue.'* He was about to tread carefully. 'Is there anything you've found, or not found, which might suggest to you that they were not killed together or at the same time?'

'You're serious?' Twite asked, frowning his non-understanding and then shrugging it off as he thought about it. 'I'd say a remote possibility; very remote. So far as my finding any free-ranging spermatozoa on the bodies is concerned they both appear to be clean, but you'll realize that death itself could be the instrument of an early coitus interruptus. Anyway, your Sergeant Magnus took their clothing for examination some time ago and if there's any seminal staining on that you'd know before me. And that'll cost you a lunch at the Quill and Gown if I have to appear at court over this,' he added with all the seriousness with which he talked about eating.

He had moved to one side of the table as he spoke and the attendant then moved to Fowler's body armed with her large curved needle and industrial thread, ready to sew it together into as much of an approximation of its original configuration as was possible.

'I'm not hooked on any of it,' Rogers said, averting his gaze from the gruesome parody of seamstressing about to be done and ignoring Twite's reference to a lunch which would lead inevitably to excessive spending. 'You know what we're like; we don't want to be caught flat-footed on any hare-brained question a defending barrister might grab out of thin air. I'm accepting that it was a case of coitus interruptus because why not? If you're caught red-handed, to speak, it so often can be.'

'And pray God it doesn't happen to either of us in the same way,' Twite whispered piously and warmly moist close to the detective's ear in deference to the susceptibilities of the attendant well within hearing distance.

That Rogers would receive a report detailing the minutiae of the examinations raised in him no expectations of resolving the question of whether the unfortunate Detective Sergeant

Henry Fowler or whatever was having what might be called a highly improper bit on the side, or doing some equally improper stuff with a drugs-dealing suspect, all for the investigative honour of Detective Chief Superintendent Gamble and his No. 12 Regional Crime Squad, was, for Rogers, very much not to the point.

# 16

Lingard liked the look of Harry Halcro, the head keeper. His rough-hewn and seamed features with his bright blue eyes – much like his own – denoted to him an honesty and decency of purpose. His strong handshake on greeting the detective was almost bone-cracking.

The working rooms he occupied were within the castle keep and opposite to the security office and the veterinary clinic. The main room hadn't much more in it than a large canteen-type table on iron stands with several wooden chairs, a row of metal clothing lockers, and floor racks occupied by pairs of spotless green wellington boots.

On one of the walls was a large black and white plan of the park and a padlocked red-painted wooden cupboard. There was a glass-panelled door through which Lingard, on entering, had seen Halcro working at a desk free of family photographs, psychotherapeutic steel balls for banging away executive neuroses, or very much in paperwork at all.

Introducing himself with his warrant card when Halcro emerged from his office, and explaining what Superintendent Rogers wanted done, Lingard said, 'I see you've had the gun cupboard padlocked.'

'Aye.' Halcro obviously hadn't worried himself into a nervous breakdown about it. 'And you might be going to say we've bolted the stable door after the horse been stolen?'

'True,' Lingard replied affably, 'though I'm not here to concern myself with too much of that. What security was there before?'

'An ordinary mortice lock and key. The problem with that was you couldn't see whether the door was locked or only shut.'

'I can take it that the key was available to your staff for use in an emergency?'

'It was kept in my office where it is now, though that doesn't mean I'm going to sit in there guarding the bloody thing any more than I could the other one.' There had been bottled-up resentment in his retort.

'Who would?' Lingard temporized. 'There's also the matter of the guns being occasionally used for shooting by your staff.' He was pinching snuff into his nose without breaking off his steady stare at Halcro.

'By two of them – for clay pigeon shooting. Mink and Baker, if you want their names.'

'I shouldn't think either would have any reason for combining that with blowing a fellow employee's head off,' Lingard commented in his most casual manner. 'Would you?'

He had watched for Halcro's reaction to that and his immediate 'Of course I bloody wouldn't,' was good enough. Good enough for the moment anyway, he thought.

'Might I see the cupboard?' he asked.

When Halcro had unhooked the red-tagged key from inside the door of his office, returning and removing the cupboard's padlock, he opened it for Lingard's inspection.

The two guns it contained, their barrels a beautiful oily blue, were stored horizontally with two hooks for a third gun below them. Small boxes of cartridges were stacked at the bottom of the cupboard.

'We haven't recovered your missing gun yet,' Lingard said, 'though we're still looking. I see you keep two different kinds of cartridges. There's a reason, I imagine?'

Halcro raised an intolerant grizzled eyebrow at the detective. 'I told your boss, chief inspector. Didn't he pass it on?'

'Briefly,' Lingard said, smiling at Halcro's testiness. 'I'm sure you're going to tell me more specifically.'

118

Halcro reached, picking up a small square box and opening it with a thumb. 'These', he explained, 'are called Triple As and, being loaded with about thirty-five pellets to the ounce, pack a heavy wallop.' He withdrew an orange-coloured cartridge, showing it to Lingard. 'They are supposed to be for putting down any large and unmanageable animal as a last resort with no other way of controlling it. So far – thank the Lord – they've not been used here for that purpose.'

Changing the box for another, he said, 'These are called number eights and they pack a load of about four hundred and fifty pellets to the ounce.' He upended the box and tapped out a blue-coloured cartridge for Lingard to see.

'They're called dust shot?'

'They're called all sorts of names, but they're number eights to me. We'd use them – again only when absolutely necessary, which hasn't happened so far – to frighten an animal or deter it in some situation less than life-threatening.'

Something in a quite unmeaning expression on Lingard's face seemed to provoke him into saying, 'Don't misunderstand me. These would only be used in an emergency and in the absence of the vet. He keeps the dart-firing pistol in his surgery to anaesthetize any animal or large bird which needs controlling. Or for surgical treatment, of course.'

'But not needing any of those cartridges to fire it, of course?'

Halcro lifted his grizzled eyebrow again. 'It's a .22 calibre pistol that fires the dart and that by an explosive charge. No pellets, no bullets; just an immobilizing dart.'

The down-put Lingard was all amiability. 'You're most helpfully explicit, Mr Halcro. Who, apart from your own staff, might have permitted access to the guns?'

'Nobody, but Security does have a key to the office, and the night man's expected to carry it in case of a fire or you name it and to check routinely for insecure windows or doors. They do for all the offices.'

'You know who that might have been last night?'

'There'd be two of them. Stoner on until two o'clock and Harris Bloor from then onwards.' The small blue eyes were questioning him. 'You think one of them?'

'Egad, no,' Lingard denied, affecting astonishment. 'Do you?'

'How would I know, man?' Halcro rasped back. 'I'm not the police.'

'You're so lucky,' Lingard murmured. 'What time are your offices vacated? At night, I mean.'

'Ten o'clock, when the night man's finished. That's now, of course, with the light evenings.'

Lingard was silent, pinching snuff from his tiny ivory box and feeding it into his sinuses. 'A favour, Mr Halcro,' he said affably. 'Mr Rogers would be grateful if you'd give him a short loan of one of the guns – he presumes the three are of the same make and choke – and two or three of each type of cartridge.'

He smiled at his own humour. 'Of course, we can't assume that he has some sort of a bird in his sights, can we? But we can always hope.'


Sergeant Flowers – Lingard could safely call her Magnolia, for he never thought of her in terms of her bosom or of any other manifestation of her massive and majestic femininity – was in a heavy red-faced sweat when he climbed the two steps into the stifling Murder Wagon and called cheerfully for any messages or information reports that had poured in during his and Rogers's absence.

Before they arrived, his fastidiousness prompted him to a wash and brush-up – and this included using the pocket toothbrush and moistening tissues he carried with him – in the telephone kiosk-sized cabinet designated for male occupancy by a black-trousered figure painted on the door.

Seated in the inadequate officer-in-command-of-operation's chair he was handed by Flowers a mud-smeared shotgun immured in a polythene membrane, the twin of that which had been handed to him by Halcro, together with a typed report from Inspector Hassell detailing its finding in the river called Dabbers Ditch some forty-five yards north-east of the summerhouse. This location he had had marked with a yellow identification post, after which he had dismissed himself and his probably exhausted and work-worn searchers for a meal and a rest period.

There had been a radio message for him, received from the Headquarters Information Room by Flowers, that said Detective Inspector Whincut of Crouch Aughton wished urgently to speak to him concerning the prisoner Laurence Stoner.

'You've dropped me and the governor of Hardenhuish eyebrow-deep in horse-shite,' a somewhat hyperbolizing Whincut told Lingard when he had got through to his office. 'The governor in particular wants to know what it was you said to an on-the-edge-of-being-reformed Stoner that he should do a runner almost as soon as you'd wiped your feet of the place. He thinks you must have said *something* that's . . .'

Lingard broke into what was promising to be something he should be taking a little seriously. 'Hang on a moment, old chap,' he said. 'Let me gather my thoughts. I know *you* don't, but do you mean the old trout's really linking chummy's escape – if he has escaped – with my having had civilized words with him?'

Whincut laughed, not wholly with humour. 'He's got to hang it on some bugger and it might just as well be you as me. He can argue that, left alone, those pampered bastards of his have no reason to go walkies – my words, not his – and I suppose we can go part of the way with him. Why should they?'

He made a noise in his throat that could be taken for hollow laughter. 'May I be forgiven for the ultimate blasphemy, but it'd never surprise me to be told that when he walked out, a prison officer opened the door for him and told him, "Good-bye, and have a nice day."'

'I can only dream up one reason,' Lingard said, being in general agreement with Whincut, 'and that is he's the man who murdered his wife and her lover last night. Not being privy to how easily Hardenhuish prisoners can get out at night unescorted, I hadn't pushed the matter of his possible involvement as much as I perhaps should.'

He paused, working things out, hearing the uninvolved and not unduly worried Whincut's soft breathing at the other end of the wire. 'I suppose I can now damn and blast the fact that I didn't,' he continued, 'knowing as I do now that he would have a sort of access through his step-brother to where the gun used for the murder was stored. I must have been brain-damaged simple,' he added in his disgust.

'Never on your life,' Whincut assured him cheerfully, being relatively on the outside of trouble and only looking in. 'While Stoner's a shiftless no-good and wholly dishonest shit, I doubt immensely that he's got the backbone to kill anyone with the hands that I know for certain haven't helped him to do a day's honest work in his life.'

'You cheer me up,' Lingard said ironically, 'and I can't believe the governor is actually after my hide.'

'Of course he isn't. I exaggerated only to show you what life's like being next door to a five-star home for misunderstood and apparently penitent prisoners.' Clearly Whincut had little time for Hardenhuish Open Prison and its occupants.

'When was he found missing?'

'Half an hour after you'd gone. He took a few personal bits and pieces and dodged joining the lunch queue.'

'He's not paying a social call in your town or in the near neighbourhood, I suppose?'

'Not a chance. He's gone all right.'

'You've circulated him?'

'Had you been in your office you'd have seen it. We know he has a passport tucked away somewhere, so I think we'll have said goodbye to him.' He didn't sound as if about to cry over it.

'If he does get picked up, we'd like first go at him.'

'It's a promise, don't worry,' Whincut said in recradling his telephone.

In replacing his own telephone, Lingard heard Sergeant Flowers in her office talking animatedly to another woman. Rising from the uncomfortable constriction of Rogers's chair

– he could feel its indentation in his buttocks – he stepped along the short passage to Flowers's office.

The caller was Lesley Wing, immaculate in her uniform of a beige-coloured epauletted shirt and slim-line skirt, being wholly pleasing to Lingard's eyes. Seen now in daylight, he wondered why he had accepted her presence at the day's dawning without experiencing the ripple of male sexual interest he now felt for this vastly attractive woman; for it had been suppressed, kept absent from the corpus of his emotions during the many years that had separated him from his lost love of poignant memory, the dead Nancy Frail.

'Mrs Wing,' he said, smiling. 'Can I help you?'

Detaching her interest from Sergeant Flowers, she smiled back at him. Impersonally? He wasn't sure. She said, 'I was to meet Mr Rogers, but he seems to be away from the park. It wasn't about anything terribly important.'

Lingard looked at his wrist-watch. 'He's almost sure to be still attending at the post-mortems. Is there anything I can do? I've a detail from him to search Harriet Stoner's room and he suggests your presence there might save a lot of argument with her brother-in-law. I'm also dealing with Stoner' brother and the one-time missing shotgun – which, incidentally, has now been recovered – if they are what you've come about.'

'I *am* interested in the shotgun, having a responsibility for the security of the gun cupboard, and certainly with backing you up in a room search. George did tell me about it.'

He showed his pleasure, prepared to latch on to anything to maintain the connection. 'It's just the job then, isn't it? Let's get out of this hothouse of a wagon and talk about it.'

Having flapped his hand at Flowers in a cheerful departure from her office, he stood outside with Lesley Wing and, with a proper lack of ostentation, indicated the magnificent-looking open-top Bentley standing greenly cool in the dappled shade of a huge oak tree. 'My old bus,' he said, appreciating that this was undoubtedly the moment for grasping firmly at the pudendum or whatever of the Goddess of Masculine Intent if there ever was to be one. 'If you could stand a possibly warm late-afternoon sherry or two while sitting in it, we could have a quite civilized conversation about searching rooms and finding guns and such things.'

She was clearly interested – and said so – both seating themselves companionably in the huge shaded Bentley. That she had no objection to drinking a sherry or two in the company of this patrician and elegant detective could be construed from her not actually saying anything against it.

Side-by-side in the car's front seats, Lingard thought his own blond and her black hair made a promising contrast, with the Yin and Yang – whatever they meant – apparently going at full steam ahead. They appeared to have worked into the ground any problem concerning the timing of the search of the dead woman's room in an ambience which, influenced by a couple of good sherries apiece that they had both happily assumed must fall short of turning green the business end of any breathalyser, somehow contained in itself the magical odours of upholstery leather soap and hot trodden-on grass.

It was then, when both had reached a friendly understanding and intimacy, that he had reached for her hand, with a little self-mockery, and brushed his lips against the back of it à la Beau Brummell, saying, 'Forgive me, Lesley, if I'm talking out of order, but from a decidedly personal interest do I have to worry about a husband who seems not to be here with you?'

It was of no particular surprise to Sergeant Flowers when she saw her favourite chief inspector – he had never looked meaningly at her bosom – walking the chief security officer of the park back to her buggy as if it were one of the nicer days of his life and then both driving away in it.


# 17


Rogers, seated with Latouche in his clinic, had insured himself against smelling of dead bodies and formalin by returning briefly to his apartment and showering with a strong-smelling body gel, then shaving – in case of a probably chancy invitation to bed by Lesley – and changing all his clothing to which, inevitably, particles of the charnel house smell would be adhering. He had then called in at his neglected office at Headquarters, avoiding being seen by Pitt-Bowsher, and checking, again unrewardingly, for any record that Angharad may have been asking for him.

Though Latouche had himself invited Rogers to the clinic, he now appeared to be uneasy, almost apprehensive, of the outcome. After offering the detective a seat and asking how he was, he was plainly finding it difficult to start on what he wished to say. He looked no happier than he had that morning.

Seen now in the still fierce afternoon sunlight slanting in through the windows and smelling of hot metal, he looked older than Rogers had earlier estimated, a little more hag-ridden. His cream-coloured hair and trim physique notwithstanding, the fine ageing lines around his dark brown eyes made him fifty years at least; though to Rogers he still looked a man likely to send married women of his own age, or even younger, into thinking seriously about the perilous delights of adultery.

Rogers, always willing to be the catalyst to garrulity, said, 'You mentioned to me on the telephone that you were performing surgery on a lioness's leg. That sounds pretty dangerous work, so I presume you'd have her well anaesthetized?'

'There's nothing dangerous about it,' Latouche told him, looking bemused at this beginning. 'I'd shot a pacifying injection into her hindquarters first. It's the paralysing drug etorphine ...' – that was how Rogers heard it – '... and it acts in two or three minutes, depending on the strength I choose, so there isn't much danger at all.'

'Nevertheless, poor lioness,' Rogers said sympathetically, having himself a quite distinct phobia against needles being thrust in different parts of his body. 'Fired from a gun?'

'By a .22 cartridge. Without a bullet in it, of course. Instead, it fires a dart about four inches long.'

'Interesting. I hope she's all right now.' He thought about it while absently stuffing tobacco into his pipe, realizing what he was doing and returning it to his pocket. 'What sort of bang does the cartridge make? Something like the shotgun cartridge you heard being shot off last night?'

'Good God, no.' Latouche looked startled. 'Nothing like it.'

'Was that what you wanted to see me about?' Rogers asked benignly, knowing it couldn't be and now wanting him to get on with what he did.

'No.' He wasn't meeting the detective's steady, almost passive stare, but was seemingly intent on the view of the chocolate-coloured castle wall from the window at his side. 'I ... I didn't tell you the whole truth about Harriet this morning and it's been worrying me. You were right in saying that I should be frank about my relationship with her.' The thin, impeccably manicured fingernails of one hand were tapping on the blotting-pad and he changed tack almost without pause. 'In any event, I don't believe I shall be here long. I'd naturally like my own practice or to be able to buy into a partnership ... deal with farm and domestic animals while there's still some mileage left in me ... you understand?'

'Not really,' Rogers said, accepting the diversion as a last-minute reluctance to admit to something he probably regarded as unpleasant or demeaning to himself. 'You were about to tell me about your relationship with Mrs Stoner. That, I believe, would be a more intimate one than that which you originally admitted?'

Latouche, pushing back strands of hair flopping down over his forehead, flushed angrily. 'Yes,' he replied stiffly, probably near to suggesting that Rogers might get stuffed, 'though perhaps you'd permit me to tell you in my own way.'

'A way in which you'd be less ambiguous and more frank than you'd persuaded me you would be?' Rogers said blank-faced.

There was silence until Latouche, fingering his mustard-coloured tie, said not too convincingly, 'I'm sorry. If I'd done something wrong, even something unlawful, perhaps I could justify my silence. What happened with Harriet wasn't correct, not under the circumstances of her employment with me. Too, I suppose her being so young and vulnerable didn't help my later regret that what I'd done was wrong and immoral.' He was silent again and Rogers was content to leave him to worry his own conscience about that.

When he had apparently done enough worrying, he said, 'I'm ashamed that I was involved with her so intimately. I'm ashamed that I'm driven to have to tell you about it.'

'When did you start employing her, Mr Latouche?' Rogers asked, not taking his crisis of conscience too seriously.

'I came to know her shortly after she arrived here. When she heard that I was in need of a secretary and assistant in the clinic, she applied.' He paused there, clearly having weighed up Rogers's reception of what he had admitted and, as clearly, thinking out his words. 'My former wife and I were divorced in Germany a decade or so ago, and were my relationship with Harriet not one of employer and employee I don't feel that it would have been the embarrassment it now is to have to admit.'

He had sounded as if he sought Rogers's assurance of perhaps the unimportance of what he had admitted. 'I don't believe – though one can never be sure – that it was known in the park,' he said, 'for I had never encouraged her to visit me in my apartment in the castle.'

'You did it in the summerhouse?' Rogers offered, deliberately crude.

Looking down his nose at the detective, in whom he was obviously disappointed, the disdain on Latouche's face was clear. 'Not in the park at all, and please don't ask me where.'

'My apologies,' Rogers murmured. 'I'm sure you were about to tell me how long this affair lasted and what caused its break-up.'

'No more than three months – it was well over a year ago – and it was my decision that it had to be ended.' He was beginning to revert to his earlier attitude of being grief-stricken. 'The poor girl . . . it wasn't my intention at all . . . was becoming intent and possessive; wanting more from me than

I could possibly give. Anyway, that was what it resulted in and after some unhappy and emotional to-ing and fro-ing we agreed that our affair was dead and, though we were to remain together, it would be as friends.'

'I see.' That disclosure hadn't set Rogers's pulse racing. Nor, as a believer in the poet Herrick's sentiments in *Gather ye Rosebuds while ye May*, was he in any position to express pious disapproval. He thought, however, that there must be something more. Making it light with a smile, he said, 'Is there anything else concerning Mrs Stoner about which you wish to be frank?'

It must have been a twitch of irritation in his face, but Latouche managed to say reasonably, 'I'm sorry. I should have told you before – I don't know why I didn't. I think I had some idea about protecting her as well as myself. She came to the clinic one morning about two months ago, fairly badly bruised on the side of her face; first of all telling me that she had tripped and fallen. This was nonsense so far as I could see and she eventually admitted that she had been beaten – she said there was bruising on her upper chest as well – by a man she had been associating with and had broken with on bad terms.'

Latouche was silent for half a brooding minute, gnawing at his lower lip, while Rogers, content to wait, had a hand in his pocket holding his filled pipe as if poised for action. He was – almost – willing to forswear his soul for a smoke.

'I feel dreadful about it now,' Latouche said, his voice low and almost a whisper. 'I might have saved her from what happened. She was crying, of course; badly upset as you'd expect. I told her I must know who the man was, that I would have what he'd done reported to the police.' His voice softened and there could have been the moistening of tears in his eyes. 'The poor frightened dear refused; refused absolutely to put a name to the inhuman brute who'd done this to her; or even to say whether he worked in the park or not. Nor', he added, 'would she visit the local surgery, accepting that I could do something for the contusions.'

'Which you did?'

He shook his head. 'I can't answer that, superintendent. I

would be in dreadful professional trouble were I to use my veterinary skills on a human being.'

'You referred to Bloor and Coope this morning,' the sceptical Rogers pointed out. 'Are you sure that Mrs Stoner, in naming those men, wasn't referring to one or the other as the man who had attacked her? Women are sometimes frightened enough not to do so. Then, remember, there's her brother-in-law. She could have had good grounds for not accusing him, being required – as she was – to live with him.'

Latouche shook his head, his eyes showing a conviction for the detective to see. 'No,' he said firmly. 'I spoke to her and I *know*. You didn't, and you don't.' He let that hang in the air and when Rogers failed to rise to it, said, 'There're other things I think I should have told you and I didn't. Whether you can accept them – or want to – as useful to what you're doing, I don't know.'

'About Mrs Stoner?' Rogers was working out a different method of encouraging information from him.

'Not as far as I can see, though it happened a day or two after she'd been beaten. When I unlocked this clinic – that'd be at nine in the morning – I found that it had been entered, obviously by someone with access to a key because the door and windows had been secure when I'd left them the previous evening. The drawers of my desk, the filing cabinet – that was unlocked anyway – and the storage and stationery cupboard had all, I thought, been rummaged through. For what, I can't honestly say, for nothing appeared to have been stolen. Or, indeed, was worth stealing.'

'Might whoever it was have been looking for your pistol?'

Latouche thought about that. 'Yes, he certainly could, though that particular night it wasn't here.' He shook his head. 'No, I can't believe that anybody would want a gun like that. It is strictly an anaesthetizer.'

'Who else has a key to the office?'

'Harriet had one and there's one in Mrs Wing's so-called guardroom.'

'Did you report all this?'

Latouche grimaced. 'No. Nor am I now reporting it to you. Nothing was stolen and it's all so damned pointless. There's nothing valuable here, and no money.' He was man of thinking pauses and he paused now. 'I'd forgotten,' he eventually said. 'There was what looked like tobacco ash on my desk.' He dabbed a finger near the edge of the desk top. 'Just here and I'm afraid I blew it off.'

'Could you tell from its shape whether it was cigarette, cigar or pipe tobacco?'

'I'm afraid not. At least, I don't think it was pipe ash. What I could see of it, it was cylindrical and perhaps thicker than cigarette ash.'

Rogers said, 'Bloody useless', under his breath without it showing in his expression, then conceding a sort of defeat and pushing back his chair, unstuck himself from the seat. Remembering the civilities, he said, 'I'm grateful, Mr Latouche, and thank you for the information you've given me.'

Outside and climbing into his baker's oven of a car, he tried to convince himself that he had not wholly been wasting his time with Latouche, not however with too much certainty. With what he thought to be a reasonably steady hand, he excused himself his haste in lighting his neglected pipe on the hot weather doing something nasty to his nerve ganglia, for which, he believed, only an immediate intake of nicotine was a prophylaxis.

Because Flash Harry Gamble had given him no help in eliminating from suspicion the known righteous in the park, he had now to add Latouche to his short list of possible drug-dealing suspects. Nor, he thought, had he heard anything to remove his growing suspicion that Latouche sported all the hallmarks of deviousness. And deviousness meant to him that there had to be something to hide; certainly Rogers felt that he had been lied to, and possibly in fairly large lumps.

# 18

To accuse Lingard of having fallen in love would be to invite derision and a flippant retort concerning fools and their poppycock delusions. But, admittedly, he was bemused about Lesley Wing, almost certain there was a strong rapport between them which was, he was certain – well, almost certain – a far different matter altogether from being in love which, accepting man's essential depravity in what was to him a materialistic world, seemed only too often to be equated with the fast shunt to a bed and mindless sexual activity.

The attraction he felt for Lesley was something more than that, though not wholly excluding it and not wholly welcomed either. A passion aroused too damn fast, he thought as he and Lesley bounced along an unmade-up road in the Prowler buggy and through the open gates of a decaying ornamental stone arch.

The headiness he felt in her presence would, he thought as a form of emotional overreach insurance, possibly – no, almost certainly – prove as short-lived and ephemeral as a migraine. He hoped so, dear Lord, but perhaps not just yet.

The village, as it had been described to him, consisted of a double row of elderly thatched cottages, none being similar in design or size to another; one at the far end had been adapted as an inn with its elaborately painted signboard inscribed 'God Bless the British Army' and describing itself as an alehouse.

The cottage at which Lesley Wing halted the buggy stood between two others, each divided from the next by a high pink-bricked wall, each having its exterior plaster lime-washed a uniform white. Stoner's cottage was thickly thatched with a growth of green lump moss on its decaying darkness which added to its appearance of being a survivor from the beginning of the century. There was an unpolished brass knocker and a numeral 3 on the sun-bleached and blistered front door. The ground floor had small lozenged windows with drab curtains which had been pulled together, giving the cottage a deserted look. A garage attached to the cottage's side wall was a modern addition and had been given a more or less matching thatch.

Lingard pulled a face as he stepped down from the Prowler. 'I don't think he's back,' he pointed out to Lesley.

'Damn,' she said, checking the time on her fob watch. 'He

should be here, if only to be readying himself for his six o'clock tour.' She shrugged. 'He could have reported direct to the guardroom, but I doubt it.'

'Could you check on your radio while I sniff around?' he suggested. 'I'd like him to be here.'

Walking the paved path to the door through a neglected garden of drooping unwatered flowers, he banged the knocker on it authoritatively, repeating it after a half-minute's non-response. Accepting that he was wasting time he rounded the cottage to its rear where a lawn and vegetable garden, neglected as much as had been the front, reached out ten yards or so to an unfenced lushly foliaged wood. The stable-type back door, divided into two, was equally unresponsive to his banging on it with his knuckles.

Looking up at the three upper windows, he could see black charring of a part of the projecting edge of the thatch above the one opened window. Stepping back to get a view of the upper thatch and frowning his puzzlement, he saw that burning had occurred in a wide sweep of the thatch's slope to where it had then died out near the ridge.

He was narrowing his eyes through a window into an untidy kitchen appearing to have an overplus of unwashed breakfast china and cutlery when Lesley with a downturned mouth rejoined him.

'Definitely not,' she said. 'The blasted man's apparently decided to make a day of it and I've had to detail Docherty for his tour.'

'A pox on't,' Lingard sounded off in a sudden irritation with the absent Stoner. 'We're wasting our time then?'

She smiled at him, dangling a tagged black mortice lock key between finger and thumb. 'Only if you've a scruple or two against using this. I've keys to all the properties, necessary it seems in cases of emergency.'

'Would you call this an emergency in your book?' She looked so overwhelmingly lovely that he wondered how he could have ever thought there would be a time when he might not want her.

'Not, but it might in yours.'

'Ah, it might well be,' he conceded, 'though it *could* be a mite dicey.' He thought it out for a little less than a couple of heartbeats, saying, 'But what the hell; it's a very much dead Mrs Stoner's room we're interested in, plus the unarguable fact that your chap happens not to be available in our hour of need.' Happily, he accepted the key. 'We are as one over this? With the onus very much resting with me, yes?'

'It's why I brought it with me,' she pointed out, clearly in accord with whatever the elegantly blond and blue-eyed Lingard might suggest.

'When we've checked the garage, I'll set course for her room and there'll be no call for you to involve yourself in something that can blow up in my face. In any case, I'll ignore his part of the house other than what I see fortuitously.'

'That's rubbish, David,' she said, not too severely. 'I've given you the key and I shall be pulling my weight as chief security officer here.'

'I'm grateful, ma'am,' he said, and he really was, giving her a slight bow as if accepting a knighthood from the Queen.

The up-and-over door to the garage was unlocked, its opening to the contained heat in it revealing an aggressively red saloon car with its engine hood propped open. A metal box of small tools lay near one of the front wheels.

Lingard touched fastidious fingers to the exposed radiator and oily cylinder head cover. 'Cold,' he said, unaccustomed sweat beading his forehead. 'Probably not used today. It *is* Stoner's?'

'I've seen him driving it almost every day.'

'It's probable non-use today is making life difficult for us, isn't it?' He was charging his sinuses with Macouba snuff, watching her face for any expression he might construe as meaning disapproval and seeing none. 'Didn't he say he was to be in Crouch Aughton or thereabouts supporting grieving relatives?'

'For what it's worth, yes. Why difficult?'

'Only in deciding how he was to get there with his car out of joint, for example. By taxi? By a borrowed car?'

She shook her head. 'By neither, I feel. He's not the type to think about a taxi. Nor, I'm sure, is he liked enough to be trusted with somebody's car.'

'So he could be inside,' he said flippantly. 'Having a quiet day off to recover? Or perhap's he's dead with rigor mortis setting in? Whichever, it makes for a difference in approach.'

Standing at the front door with Lesley at his back, he lifted the tarnished knocker and banged it down twice, hard enough to make the door shudder. Immediately lifting open the letter flap and stooping to it, he listened without result for sounds of movement. He did it again, hearing from inside the same nothingness, then pushing Lesley's key in the lock and turning it.

Inside the hall in the stuffy reddish twilight of drawn together curtains, he could smell what he thought to be the after-ghost of a fried bacon breakfast. A partly open door on the left of the steep and narrow stairs facing them showed dimly a sitting-room overcrowded with furniture and in which he cautiously felt he could take no official interest.

'Direct to Mrs Stoner's room if we can find it, and if you still insist on involving yourself,' he said, climbing the stairs to a sunlit first-floor landing. In it there were three distressingly modern plywood doors stained a dark brown; one on his immediate left and two in a short uncarpeted passage on his right. He opened the first door, it being immediately and obviously a woman's bedroom.

Standing aside for Lesley to enter, he said, 'Could I leave the more intimate of her possessions to you? Anything you find connecting her to any person in the park might be useful. Even something concerning her husband, and definitely any sighting of her missing handbag, of course.'

He looked around at the low-ceilinged room, initially seeing a substantial bolt on the inside of the door which reflected ill on Stoner's supposed sexual incapacity. There was a single bed with a barred metal bedhead, made up neatly enough other than that its two pillows had been disturbed and a shortie white nightdress, which could have been with them, was now lying carelessly on the once polished planked floor. A small bedside table held a paper-shaded lamp, a short row of paperback novels and a framed photograph of a curly-haired man with a black Italian moustache.

Against one wall was a 1930s-style bulbous wardrobe, and underneath the single small window, lace-curtained and with flies buzzing hysterically against it for release, stood a triple-mirrored dressing-table fitted with four narrow drawers. It was a depressing room, Lingard thought; as hot as hell and stuffy; certainly not one in which a civilized man could be happily entertained.

First opening the window and releasing the flies, he said, 'I'd be grateful if you'd do the drawers, though I've a suspicion we've been beaten to it by Stoner. I think I'll be safely unembarrassed in doing the wardrobe and having a look at the bed.'

At the finely drawn finish of the search there had been found nothing in the room to indicate that the occupant of it had been anything but an hotel-staying transient, though with a larger amount of clothing, nightwear and scents and make-up toiletries than the average.

In particular, there was no handbag, shoulder bag or clutch bag and Lingard guessed confidently enough that it wasn't going to be found in the cottage or anywhere else. Had there been any notes or documents, any indication of an active sexual life or even of any connection with her employment by Latouche – and he thought that there had to be – he and Rogers had been forestalled by whatever concealment or disposal had taken place.

'Damn,' he said to the enchanting Lesley. 'You'd think there'd be something that the bastard had overlooked, wouldn't you?'

'You believe it was Stoner who killed her? Not, say, her husband?'

'Ah,' he said, suddenly unhappy, smacking the palm of his hand against his forehead. 'I hadn't got around to putting you in the picture because I haven't yet seen George and given him an update on events. I suppose it's more or less confidential stuff until I have, but I've a good case for telling you now that our other Stoner went walkabout from Hardenhuish Open Prison early this afternoon. While I can't rule out the possibility that he's hightailing it for foreign parts, he could be making an idiot of me and be somewhere in the vicinity of the park with a dark intent.'

She had raised her eyebrows at this. 'I didn't know he was even in prison, and I'm surprised that Harriet had never told me. Have you seen him? To tell him about her death?'

'I'm only just back from knowing he was there. *And* he'd already been told by the prison governor.' He pushed more Macouba into his apparently demanding sinuses. 'Not that he took it all that sorrowfully; not that he appeared to want to tear somebody's liver out over it either.'

'So he couldn't have had anything to do with killing Harriet then?'

Choosing his words carefully, he said, 'A shrewd assessment, Lesley, but not quite so. Given the criminally loose supervision that's given its freedom at the prison, I believe it quite possible that he could leave it at night much as he wished. Of course, that leaves access to the shotgun rather hanging.'

'He could get it through his brother.'

'Indeed he could,' he agreed, shying away from anything concerning Stoner's walk-out from the prison. 'I have a feeling, an instinct, that I should now move away from the brief I've been landed with. Legally or illegally, I'm going to look through the other rooms.' He was serious with her behind his amiability, returning her direct stare. 'I don't want to lose you, but it might be proper if you returned outside and did not associate yourself too closely with a tortfeasor-to-be.'

'I wouldn't dream of it,' she retorted in a manner suggesting that she wouldn't be argued with. 'At the worst we can be held in contempt or something like it.' She wasn't taking him at all seriously.

'A lovely thought,' he smiled at her, 'but I'll still convince myself that I'm on my own.'

Out of the bedroom, he opened the first of the other two doors, finding it to be a combined lavatory and bathroom, nothing in it exciting his interest. The remaining door opened into the untidiness of a no-longer-married man's bedroom, uninviting in its lack of anything but an unmade double bed, a chest of drawers with an ashtray of dog-ends on its top and a doorless wardrobe of male clothing. The room smelled strongly of stale cigarette smoke, the ceiling beginning to turn brown from it.

Its window was that which he had seen to be open from the outside and he went to it, looking out of it and up at the overhang of the blackened thatch. Reaching it with his arm was easy and, if attempted arson it had been, then he couldn't think of any reason why the dried straw or reed used in it hadn't gone up in massive flame. Or, indeed, a reason for Stoner to do it.

Downstairs, entering the sitting-room and switching on the light against the curtained dimness, Lingard confirmed his first impression of overcrowdedness. Among other smaller pieces of furniture was a dining-table with three chairs, two twin-seat sofas, three over-padded easy chairs and a high-backed wing chair turned away from him and facing the rear curtained window with a television set under it showing a red warning light at its base.

It wasn't that which caused Lingard to stand dumbstricken in a paralysis of inertia, but the sticking out from the base of the chair of two feet wearing soiled white trainer shoes, somehow unsettling in their stillness.

Bereft of speech and clear thinking at the sheer unexpectedness of it in the few stretched-out seconds it took, his brain threw up wildly improbable reasons and excuses for being where he was and why the bloody unreasoning hell hadn't Stoner answered his knocking and done something civilized about their coming in and rummaging about upstairs like a couple of criminous housebreakers instead of sitting there in a goddamned trance and allowing them to finish up with a growing and justifiable anger at the stupid and probably mind-blown unheeding prat.

Then, having failed to find a not too improbable reason for forcing his way into somebody else's house – hearing as if amplified the silent Lesley's breathing behind him – it hit him as suddenly as had his seeing them that the feet had an unnatural stillness about them; not that of sleep, nor of unconsciousness, but only of the unmistakable inertness of death.

In four strides he was at the chair, seeing death in one of its more violent and horrible forms, waving back Lesley who was about to follow him, and recovering his composure, his momentarily fled *savoir-faire*.

But he was reading things in the dead body – he wasn't about to test the presence or absence of life in a man so manifestly a corpse – that didn't accord with Rogers's pungent description of Stoner. This was a younger man with a young man's bigness dressed in the ill-fitting trousers and shirt which seemed to mean that he had been sartorially 'with it'. He was now a young man with a distorted, bulging-eyed and suffused face. He had died with a flashily patterned tie sunken tightly in the flesh of the throat.

Examining him further, Lingard noted the disordered hay-coloured hair, the girlish mouth from which an inch of mauve-coloured tongue protruded stained in one corner with an effusion of pinkish fluid, and the profusion of tiny haemorrhages in the eyes and in the livid flesh. A pair of steel-rimmed glasses had fallen on to his stomach, lodging in a fold of his trousers.

Touching the backs of his fingers to the face and flexing one of the limply hanging arms, he decided for himself that he mightn't have been dead for much more than an hour or two, or even three.

He beckoned Lesley to him. 'Do you mind, poppet? He's very much dead and I don't believe he can be your chap Stoner.'

She was, he thought, an eminently cool and intelligent presence to have in support in moments when the brain swam and the blood ran cold. No floundering, no vapours or unwelcome hysteria. 'Strangled by ligature as you may see,' he told her, 'and I've little doubt that you'll be able to tell me who he is.'

'Quentin Coope,' she said with a woman's sadness, 'and he's working out his time as a temporary keeper until he goes up to university. George interviewed him in my office this afternoon.'

Lingard looked at his watch. It was near six thirty. 'As one of Mrs Stoner's reputed lovers, I'd guess?'

She hesitated. 'I don't know how to say this, David, but I'd rather you asked George himself. I'm restricted in my official capacity here as much, I imagine, as are you in yours.'

He could almost see the lieutenant's bronze stars on the epaulettes of her shirt and was impressed. He was also somewhat shamefaced, wanting to kick himself. 'I'm sorry. I really am. It was thoughtless of me.'

She smiled at the elegant detective in the beautifully tailored summer suit whom she had already decided, the Fates being willing, to be hers. 'Anything else,' she said, 'and I'll tell you or help you.'

'You're a poppet and I love you for it,' he said extravagantly in the rush of blood to his head, gently taking her arm and leading her away from the dead youth. 'You have the wheels as they say, and I'd love you even more if you'd toddle off and hunt down our respected George as a matter of urgency, briefing him on this lot.' He laughed at the picture coming into his mind. 'Be sure to be quick on your feet when you've done it, or you'll know what it's like to be stuck in the path of a charging buffalo.'

Once outside and releasing her arm, looking around at the apparently deserted village, he kissed the back of her hand again and said, '*A bientôt*, poppet. It's now my sad duty to stay here and brood on the whys and wherefore of that poor bugger inside until George comes steaming up.' He looked into her eyes and was pleased with what he saw. 'If you can, save the evening for me, would you? I've a pressing need for a decent meal in pleasant company in Abbotsburn.'

With Lesley having departed silently in her buggy – in Lingard's view it was something synonymous with the sun vanishing behind a cloud – it prompted him into an acceptance that life was, as had been the life of the now horribly dead youth, an uncertain and possibly transient thing. One day he was going to be as dead as Coope, finishing up as a worm's dinner; and dammit, why should he contemplate leaving life, sordid, dirty and treacherous as it was, without having tasted to the full of its few pleasures and sweetnesses?

The resolution stayed with him like a remembered smile, though not so long that ten minutes later it interfered with his finding of a rolled-up bloodstained tunic shirt and trousers stuffed behind the wardrobe in Stoner's bedroom. That, and his now settled opinion that only the owner of a smooth unwrinkled brain could have lived in the cottage with its lack of anything likely to engage the intellect.

# 19

An exhausted Rogers was in a condition near to suspended animation. It was close to eight o'clock and he had now been unrested for fifteen hours non-stop following the disturbed three hours' sleep the previous night; then called from bed more tired than when he had got into it. His eyes were tired too, everything and everybody looking either greyly uninteresting or tiresome, his inner being waxing apathetic.

Professional pride made his tiredness – it had now almost stopped him dead in his tracks – nothing to which he would admit, though these were times when he wished he had guided his future into painting beautiful women or, a poor second, into the well-salaried unexcitability of chartered accountancy at which he had once been pointed.

He was rather less than excited as he walked with Lingard at the rear of the fled Stoner's cottage, discussing the death of Coope and Stoner's almost certain guilt, while staying out of the way of the Coroner's officer and his required removal of the dead youth in one of the coffin shells which furnished the inside of his anonymous-appearing goods van.

Everything that needed to be done had been done: the laid-down routine for discovered murder had been activated by Lingard on what was to prove a dead evening with most everybody fleeing the day into unobtainability. Pitt-Bowsher, the Assistant Chief Constable, had been informed and had as promptly said that he was in effect champing at the bit to be at the scene if he could only back out from an important conference and dinner he just had to attend, but anyway having every confidence in the department's handling of it should he not be able to get away. A message had been left for a wisely off-duty and an unable-to-be-found Dr Twite that a body would shortly be waiting on him in the mortuary; and the attendance of a long-suffering Detective Sergeant Magnus had been ordered to photograph the body *in situ*, together with the evidence of the attempted arson, then to pack and preserve Stoner's bloodstained clothing for delivery to the Forensic Science Laboratory the following morning.

Then, it having been assumed that Stoner was almost certainly involved – this was a saving grace – in the three murders, his name and description were circulated country wide as being Wanted Most Urgently for Questioning by Detective Superintendent G. Rogers of the Abbotsburn Police, with the suggestion – a wild and unsubstantiated guess this – that he might possibly be found in the company of his stepbrother, Laurence Stoner, an escapee from Hardenhuish Open Prison. In fact, both detectives thought that William Stoner must be somewhere not too far from the park, hiding out in a cold sweat and most likely being subject to a guilty man's loosening of the bowels.

If there was anything else that needed doing, Rogers decided that it would have to wait until the morning.

The grass he and Lingard trod and which appeared to have once been a lawn had been dried by the summer's sun to frizzled hay, each footfall of their walking sending up small clouds of swarming insects and pollen dust. It was a sweat-drop or two less hot, the setting sun being dimmed by a gathering of ground mist, the precursor of the much disliked summer sea fog that could roll inland in a blindness of damp obscurity.

'I'd seen young Coope this afternoon,' Rogers was telling Lingard, 'and I thought then that he was holding back something about his moth hunting near the summerhouse last night. Something like a cover-up of what he'd seen or heard sort of thing; of that I'm sure.' He held back what could have been a jaw-breaking yawn. 'I think now he'd seen Stoner – or thought he had – leaving there, though not probably taking any particular notice of him. I don't believe there could be more than that or he'd have reported it. Seeing Stoner leaving the summerhouse wouldn't have been anything unusual, not until this morning when he was told that it had been the scene of a couple of brutal murders.'

He struck a match, sucking its flame into the bowl of his pipe, irritably flapping smoke away from his face. 'It was then, I think, that he made his ill-judged venture into criminal extortion. For a young chap with a vicar for a father it seems a surprising venture, but no more I suppose than others with which we've dealt. Bloody fool,' he said absently, thinking more of the supposed drugs operation than the actual killing of Fowler and Mrs Stoner. 'He was always out of his depth.'

'I'd not met him, of course,' Lingard said, 'and I wouldn't know the type but, unless he was involved in the murders as a jolly old accessory, I can't imagine another motive for his killing. You're happy about the attempted arson? Friend Stoner trying to cover himself after killing chummy?'

'Yes. Attempted only because there's a special fire retardant they splash on thatched roofs now and that's something he should have known.'

'Or chose to ignore. Panic stations and all that. It's not every day you're required to strangle somebody with a terribly ill-chosen tie in order to shut him up.'

Rogers tapped his teeth with the stem of his pipe, feeling even that to be a hell of an effort, and seeing Lingard's patrician features as not quite so clear-cut and well-scrubbed as he knew they must be. 'It might be significant that Coope is the second of Mrs Stoner's lovers to be picked off,' he said, suspecting that he was rather mumbling his words.

Seeing no sign of agreement from Lingard, he let that one slide. 'No, I suppose not. Let's rethink the necessity that drove Stoner after we've slept on it.' Sleep, he thought. Lovely annihilating unconsciousness in bed before he shamed his masculinity by falling flat on his face.

'Laurence Stoner,' Lingard reminded him. 'I can't believe going walkabout from Hardenhuish so near to the finish of his sentence wasn't something to do with his wife's death.'

'There's a connection. There has to be.' And if there was, Rogers considered that it could be connected with the trafficking in drugs that was hidden from them and not primarily with his wife's having it off with so many of the male staff at the park. 'Have a guess how,' he suggested.

'That his attitude towards her was something he put on for my benefit?' Lingard reflected on that for no more than a second or two. 'No,' he said. 'At a pinch, with some suspension of belief, I can see him getting out of Hardenhuish last night, getting hold of the shotgun with the help of his stepbrother, doing something about the dishonour ...' – he laughed at his saying of it – '... his so-called wife was bringing on himself and on his illustrious family and then creeping back to chokey. Somehow though, I can't believe it. Certainly not to return today in daylight and adventitiously get around to strangling the unfortunate Coope.'

Rogers was equally unimpressed. 'I'm putting my money on his stepbrother. How did Halcro take the news? Coope being his lodger and under his tutelage so to speak.'

'Cut up, of course, but there's nothing from him that'd help.'

'No, I wouldn't think Coope was the sort of chap to open up about anything remotely dodgy to a hard-cased moralist, landlord or not. And before I forget it, would you give Mrs Wing my apologies and would she cancel the shooting test I'd arranged for later this evening. With Stoner on the trot it won't be necessary.' It was then that his tiring brain threw up what he thought might be an important incongruity. There was no blaze of clarifying light, but certainly a something into which he could dig his investigating teeth.

'She hadn't mentioned it,' Lingard drawled, though looking surprised and slightly challenging. 'In fact I'd arranged to take her out for a rather special beefburger with fries and a small Coke on the side at Throckmortens Eating House this evening.'

There was a longish silence in which they could hear the coughing grunts of a big cat; probably a pacing lion complaining about the unusual heat.

'Good,' Rogers said, smiling through his teeth and lying, wishing he could have afforded without wincing a sitting or two at the hideously expensive Throckmortens. 'I hope you both enjoy it. And return the spare gun and cartridges to Halcro, will you?'

He knew, had suspected, that Lesley had gone off him, though he hadn't suspected that his second-in-command would so quickly take over she whom he had marked out for himself. He was so far gone in tiredness – he felt his eyelids hanging heavily, feeling as if some of the thickening sea fog had crept into his skull – that he wasn't as frustrated, as irritated, as he might have been earlier on.

With Lingard watching him – he thought, quizzically – he said, 'I'd better get back to the office, David, and leave the rest to you. I've some neglected writing to do and to see the ACC if I can catch the bugger in and update him. I've no doubt he'll be bloody querulous about my not anticipating that Coope was about to be strangled.'

In his car, pulling out on to the road back to Abbotsburn, his view through the already dusty windscreen was diminished by the sinking sun's refraction and the so far thinly smothering mist that the locals called a steaming-pot fog. That, he thought, or his eyes' retinas were understandably knocking off work for the day.

It decided him, if he made it back to Abbotsburn without carving himself up in an accident, to make a miss of processing a preliminary progress report or conferring with an only-might-be-available Pitt-Bowsher. Also, he had the matter of

Stoner's apparently unarguable guilt to think about, and of the apparent irreconcilability of last night's single gunshot.

In his apartment, suitable, he had always considered, only for non-claustrophobic dwarves, Rogers poured himself a generous single malt whisky and why not for he wasn't going out again that night. Sipping at it, he tapped out his Headquarters number. Even that had been an effort of concentration.

It had been worth it. A call from a Mrs Angharad Rhys Pritchard had been logged and a message form had been left on his office desk asking him to telephone her that evening. Just that, with Lesley forgotten and, despite his desperate tiredness, his loins reacting warmly; or he thought that they would have had he not been so physically bushed.

Calling her number and sipping again at the comforting whisky, he waited on the calling signal, knowing very soon, always knowing anyway when a telephone was ringing in an unoccupied room, that it wasn't going to be answered.

His mood reverting to an unusual dark shade of grey, he recradled the receiver, undressed and took a steaming shower to spray the odours of death and summer sweat from his body and hair.

Towelling himself dry in front of a steam-misted mirror, he was ruefully unimpressed by the man reflected in it; a black-haired man appearing to be in his desperately late sixties – though he felt like one in his eighties – with the eyes pouched, the sallow skin sagging and creased with tiredness, and the chin and jowls darkly stubbled; the picture of a man, he believed, who would understandably be shrugged off by a beautifully tight-skinned attractive woman such as Lesley.

He was in a mood to wish he could arrange a posting to Ulan Bator or anywhere in Outer Mongolia for his friend and colleague Lingard who had, almost certainly unknowingly, somehow inserted his elegant self between Rogers and Lesley and snatched her from almost under his unaware nose.

Not too happy, naked as a peeled banana and allowing his brain to go into free fall, he belly-flopped on to his unmade bed and was immediately gone.

## 20

The repetitive ringing of his bedside telephone woke Rogers from his almost death-like sleep, his gathering awakeness merging into a furious anger. Reaching out an arm which felt heavy and nerveless, he pushed the receiver from its cradle without lifting it and said into the darkness of the room, 'For Christ's sake, what the bloody hell is it now?' while trying to think what time it might be and wasn't there ever to be any peace on this falling-apart sodding earth other than in the grave.

Hearing a squawking from the receiver – he thought it might even be an on-the-job Pitt-Bowsher though that wasn't worrying him overmuch – he picked it up and croaked, 'Who is it, and what's the time?'

'Sir,' the voice said, sounding rather peeved, 'it's Inspector Orris and it's 11.10 p.m. I've a fatal I've been asked to pass to Mr Lingard or to you by Inspector Bragg from Thurnholme. I tried to get hold of Mr Lingard but he's away from his rooms and I'm sorry I've had to disturb you. Inspector Bragg's now at Castle Caldbeck Park dealing with a man killed by a tiger. He's William Stoner, a security guard employed there and he's the chap who's been circulated as wanted and . . .'

'For God's sake!' Rogers interrupted him. 'I know all that. When was this?'

'I've only just been told, sir,' the offended Orris replied, thinking, what was it with these bloody superintendents? 'But he's certainly only been found inside the half-hour.'

'Was the tiger outside its enclosure?'

'I don't know, sir. It didn't sound like it.'

'Right.' Rogers had more or less – less, he felt – put himself together, though something had triggered off the beginning of a thumping headache. 'Notify Mr Lingard if he ever gets back tonight, but in the meantime get Mr Coltart to meet me at the park with a couple of bodies, the Coroner's Officer and Detective Sergeant Magnus in case I need them. And before all that, send me round a patrol car straight away. I'm probably over the top with a double whisky malt inside me and in no condition to do my own driving.'

Distinctly unrefreshed by about two and a half hours' sleep, he dressed himself in a hurry without a ritual washing, simultaneously wondering with a tired brain how in the hell a murderous bugger like Stoner could get himself killed by a tiger who was presumably secure in the high-fenced and ditched enclosure he had seen earlier that afternoon, which now seemed like months ago.

Outside in the patrol car – a dark, deserted and dead outside with only policemen and other bloody idiots unsleepingly abroad – and heading for the wildlife park, he stuffed the remaining shreds of his tobacco in his pipe and lit it, ignoring purposely the Chief Constable's edict that his No Smoking rule applied to Constabulary vehicles as well as offices and, in his present mood, to hell with that.

While the more harsh-tasting tobacco smoke brought no relief to his thumping headache, he believed that it brought a touch of normality into his almost sleepless existence, mellowing somewhat any irritation or short-temperedness he might otherwise feel.

A few miles short of Castle Caldbeck, the car entered the obscurity and warm dampness of the steaming-pot fog which had rolled inland from the sea. It wasn't as dense as it could be, but it did limit visibility to ten or so yards; certainly not sufficiently so that the bearded security guard Bloor, passing the patrol car through the already opened public entrance gate, had any difficulty in recognizing Rogers and giving him a sardonically mock salute as it was driven through.

Having passed through the spaced-out avenue of small fog-shrouded subfusc blue moons which were the mercury-vapour lamps needed by poor Coope for his moth hunting and reaching the enclosure where he had paused to admire the beautiful tigress, he had the car pulled to a standstill in a spur off the road and near the small group fiercely illuminated by a loudly hissing floodlamp. Behind them was the impenetrable blackness of the building presumably housing the tigers and nearby the large skeletal frame of the enclosure's gate. Adjacent to the fencing was a zebra-striped four-wheel drive wagon, a park security buggy in its mourning black and a small police runabout, all gleaming with the fog's moistness.

Dismounting and feeling oddly that the fog was pressing down on him with a moist impalpability, Rogers approached the group standing in the cavern of white light and black shadows, recognizing Bragg the Thurnholme Bay uniformed inspector and Harry Halcro the time-worn, seamed and veinous-nosed head keeper.

Behind the group, standing unnoticed in the shadow of the wagon, was a large woman in a security guard's uniform – obviously, he considered, the Kate Docherty who Lesley had said hadn't to wear trousers in order to be a good security officer – and a youngish man wearing a leather anorak who was probably one of Halcro's keepers. On the ground behind the wagon was a plastic tarpaulin-covered flat-on-its-back body with its shod feet exposed and pointing up to the unseen sky.

There was what Rogers would later recall as a breathless-hush atmosphere about their waiting, as though something almost epochal had happened or was about to happen. As an accompaniment to the macabre tableau, he could hear a deep-throated growling, an intermittent rumbling coming from the ill-defined enclosure with its dark clumps of shrubbery and, possibly as an extension to his fraught imagination, the half-glimpsed moving insubstantiality of a giant cat padding its restlessness at the edge of his perception.

'Good evening,' he said to the group with a put-on geniality that almost hurt, and beckoned Bragg to him. 'First things first,' he explained, 'and I'd like to be put in the picture first by the inspector.'

It wasn't much, but enough in a form made concise by Rogers's requirement for pithiness. Bragg had received an emergency call from Mrs Kate Docherty, the duty security officer, that an unknown man had been heard by her to be in the tigers' enclosure and had been attacked, almost certainly mauled to death. Mr Halcro, the head keeper, was in attendance and arranging for the body – if there was one – to be recovered.

When he, Bragg, had arrived at the scene, Mr Halcro and his assistant had already entered the enclosure in their range wagon and were driving out through the gate with the body of the man on board. He himself had seen and heard one of the tigers inside the enclosure, but nothing more. When the badly mutilated body had been unloaded from the wagon, it had been immediately identified as William Stoner, one of the park's security guards, by both Mr Halcro and Mrs Docherty.

He had brought a PC with him who was now in the process of doing a check of the wire mesh fence to see whether entry had been affected by cutting it or even by climbing it, though that seemed unlikely in view of the fence's height of fifteen feet.

When Rogers asked Bragg if Mrs Wing the chief security officer had been notified – he had made it a quite casual question – Bragg had said no, Mrs Docherty had told him that she had left the park earlier that evening and was off duty. Rogers could accept that, for there was little doubt that Lingard had taken her out for what he had facetiously called a beefburger and a coke, either of which would have been totally unfamiliar to his epicurean taste.

Bragg had finished his report by saying that though a number of the park's employees had been to the scene, he had made it his business to persuade all the merely morbidly curious to leave, though these did not include the veterinary, Mr Latouche, and the security guard Bloor.

'Hang on and wait until I get some more troops here,'

Rogers told him, then approached the three who were waiting near the body.

'An unwelcome intruder I hear,' he said to Halcro who was chewing around an unlit cheroot. 'You've identified him, I'm told?'

'It's Stoner all right,' he growled. The white light from the floodlamp was cutting deep shadowed grooves in his face, his hair and eyebrows glistening with condensation. 'It wasn't Lalapur's fault. The bastard – speak no ill of the dead – had no right to be in there. I thought he'd be gone after what he'd done to young Coope.' He sounded deeply bitter.

'Yes,' Rogers said noncommittally. 'And Lalapur's the tiger?'

'The tigress, and she's got cubs. What could anyone expect?' He was already on the defensive and poised to be aggressive.

'I agree. Don't think I'm on anything but the tiger's side.' He was fighting a need to do something else but yawn behind clenched together teeth.

Apparently mollified, Halcro said, 'Her mate is Rajah, and he's a softie. He wouldn't hurt a fly. She wouldn't either unless she felt her cubs were being threatened.'

Rogers stepped towards the bulky shape under the plastic, lifting its end and exposing the dead face to the light. He had seen Stoner for a few minutes only that morning, but his Cro-Magnon physiognomy and ginger whiskers were unmistakable. Rogers thought extravagantly that he looked rather unhappy about being dead, the left side of what had been his throat being a mangled bloody mess in which could be seen the pinkish-white ends of ruptured cartilage in the windpipe. During the few moments that he contemplated the unsettling fact of a violent death, it had crept into his mind that this could be Harriet Stoner's justifiable revenge brought about from another dimension to which she had so prematurely gone. He hoped that it was.

'He lost an arm somewhere in there,' Halcro said over Rogers's shoulder, 'and there's no way it's coming out to-night.'

Rogers pulled the heavy plastic further down, and even that

took some effort by his weary body. The whole left arm had been messily torn from its socket and, with it, the sleeve of the shirt that Stoner's body was wearing.

'I wasn't about to suggest that either of us should go in and look for it,' he said amiably. He straightened his legs, a painful readjustment of bone and muscle making soft cracking noises as he lifted upright the ton-and-a-half that his body now felt it weighed. 'I'll have further words with you if you'll wait, as I'd like to start with Mrs Docherty and let her get on with making the park safe for civilization.'

'What about *him*?' Halcro jerked his head at the body in its plastic winding sheet. 'I think the cats know he's still here and Rajah's not going to settle down until he's gone.' He had lit his rank-smelling cheroot and he spat out a fragment of tobacco leaf. 'He *is* the right bloke, isn't he?'

'You mean about the death of young Coope?'

'Of course I do. He lived with us and whatever his connection was with that brute Stoner he didn't deserve to die for it.'

'Chief Inspector Lingard spoke to you about it, I imagine?'

'He said he was found strangled to death in Stoner's cottage with Stoner gone missing so it doesn't take much thinking about who did what, does it? I mean, the whole bloody park knows what happened and who did it.' Beneath his irritation, if that was what it was, he seemed to be deeply unhappy about Coope's death.

'A terrible tragedy all round,' Rogers said. 'So far as Stoner's body is concerned – and we don't want it to stay here for too long – it'll be taken away when it's been photographed and when the Coroner's Officer arrives.' He was dodging giving an opinion on Stoner's guilt and moved away from the death of Coope. 'You don't think it was Rajah who killed him?'

'No, I don't. I saw Lalapur when we were in there and she had blood on her jaws. Rajah's just doing his guardian male act after the event. He's arthritic anyway and would have been dead by now in his natural habitat. He's zoo-bred anyway, which means he's used to his keepers and suchlike, and a great big softie like I said. So is Lalapur normally, though when she has cubs to protect that doesn't go with making her cuddly; not even with her particular keepers and she normally loves them.' He shook his head, being deadly serious. 'That daft bugger was asking for it and he got it. But nobody's going to get away with blaming my cats.'

'I'm not in the business of blaming her for anything, Mr Halcro,' Rogers said mildly, holding back from facetiously saying he thought God or somebody in charge of earthly misdemeanours and so forth had dished out a suitably signposted punishment with which he agreed. There wasn't in his opinion much point in saying 'Thou shalt not kill' if nothing much was done about it when the commandment, or whatever it was, was flouted. 'I'll see you again about the enclosure's security in a few minutes,' he promised.

He shook hands with the impressive Kate Docherty, much taken with her. She was, even taking into consideration the glaring light of the hissing floodlamp and the extreme tiredness of his perception of things on a dismally fogbound night, a big and voluptuous woman; Rogers judged her of operatic Brünnhildean proportions and she wore her security guard's tunic and skirt with élan. She had a mane of tawny hair, a face of unexpected classic beauty and appeared to be cheerful and unshaken, even unmoved, by what had happened.

'I've been about the park all day,' he said, 'but not happening to have met you. You'd taken over Stoner's shift?'

'If you think about it, and of course you must have, my being here and standing in for him when he was killed shows it. Still, it was an odd mischance, wasn't it? For him, at least.'

She radiated a huge kindliness with a voice which was strong and pleasantly modulated. Rogers knew that his much younger sex-hungry self would have lusted to have been enfolded, however painfully and possibly ineffectually, in her mighty arms.

'Tell me about it, Mrs Docherty,' he asked her, trying to look clear-eyed and vigorous and praying that his unshaven stubble would be concealed from her in dark shadow; a man not admitting to aching muscles and creaking bones and a tired not-quite-with-it mind. 'What time did it all happen?' He thought her eyes were a dark green, certainly a dark something.

'Twenty-past ten exactly,' she said. 'I was on my way in the Prowler to my point at the restaurant where I was due at ten thirty and there was a dirty fog like there is now, but the lights were on and that helped so when I was passing quite near the tigers' enclosure – lovely darling puss-cats, aren't they? – I heard this dreadful screaming; anyway a man's screaming I thought, though I wasn't sure, coming from somewhere near the enclosure.'

Her eyes were showing something that could have been the memory of the emotional impact of the moment. She continued, 'when I got there, which was pretty damn quick I can tell you, I could just see one of those beautiful cats through the fog and he was holding this man by his arm which was in his mouth and he'd stopped crying out, though I couldn't tell whether he was dead or not or even moving and I could only just see the other cat standing further in the fog near the big tree trunk there and not doing anything but watching.'

She had got that out in a bit of a rush, her phrasing promising volubility, though with none of the Irishness her name might suggest, and Rogers grunted his acceptance of it and for her to get it all out.

'I was going to say I had this flashlight out . . .' – she rapped a finger on the long black barrel of it strapped to her tunic belt – '. . . and I shone it at the tiger I saw standing over the man with one paw on him and growling at me and then padding off until I couldn't see him which wasn't very far off.'

'You know there's a male and female in there, do you?'

'Yes, but I wouldn't know which one even if I saw them together and would it make any difference which one it was who killed him which seems to me he must have wanted, though why he yelled like he did about it when it happened I wouldn't know.'

'Perhaps it was beginning to hurt him, being chewed at by a tiger,' he said, not wholly serious. 'Go on.'

'There's not much else. I sounded off the siren we carry in the buggy for important emergencies with the animals and sat there to calm myself down while I waited for Harry who came running from the staff bar with two of his keepers who went back for their wagon when I told them what I'd seen and heard. Then they came back with the wagon and Harry had a gun and I called out to him that I'd hate him to hell and back if he hurt the cats and he shouted back something I didn't hear and which I suppose was just as well. Then they went into the enclosure and I couldn't look at what they were doing though I heard Harry cursing and being a bit angry and then it was I got out of the buggy and went to the gate, bawling out to him not to hurt them and being a funny man . . .' – she laughed, showing more teeth than a normal woman would reasonably have – '. . . he called out telling me and probably everybody in earshot to shut up and to stop peeing in my knickers for nobody was going to be hurt, and then they came out in the wagon and Harry said it was William Stoner's body, the very man I was standing in for.'

When she paused and he thought she had finished, he was framing words to ask her about Stoner when off she went again. 'Anyway, Harry asked me if I would identify Stoner as he wanted to be sure and I looked at him when he was still in the back of the wagon and of course it was the wretched man himself and no mistaking him. I'll say this, he certainly looked no worse than he had before he went in there and God only knows why the stupid man went in there in the first place though as I said it was probably what he wanted to do . . .' – her face was suddenly hard and cruel – '. . . for whatever it was he's done to that poor boy.'

'He's not one of your friends, I gather?' Rogers suggested, having tried to partition her verbiage into coherent sentences and believing she was working herself into a fume about men's inherent idiocies.

She tossed her magnificent tawny hair. 'It's the truth,' she said, 'but if it had to be anybody, I'm glad it was him and may God forgive me but he was a nasty brute and poorly pathetic with it.'

'Pathetic?' Rogers queried, not yet having heard anyone expressing pity or sympathy for the brutish Stoner who seemed not to be any better thought of for being dead anyway.

'Yes, the way he treated his wife poor woman and her being a bit lacking in her brain if you know what I mean and with Harriet who should have known better than to stay in the same house with him.'

'Why do you think he climbed in the enclosure under his own steam?'

'How else would he be in there?' she said with clear feminine logic. 'I wouldn't know and I don't believe anybody else would either and not when you know what a bloody-minded and filthy beast he could be.'

'I have to doubt that he ever was with you,' he said, careful to put complete disbelief in his words.

Her scorn was massive. 'Don't ever think it,' she said sharply. 'I'd have choked the brute myself and a lot more unpleasantly than the tiger did.'

It wasn't in Rogers's nature to accept that what she was saying was necessarily the truth. 'I suppose there'll be someone here to weep for him?' he suggested, doing a little fishing.

'They'd be fools if they did,' she said, still scornful of the dead man and that, as Rogers had to accept, was very much that. He had noticed her looking over his shoulder at her standing buggy, probably champing at the bit to be off, he thought. 'Before you go,' he said, 'did you know young Coope at all?'

'Of course I did. He lodged with us.'

'He did?' he said blankly. 'I thought he lodged with Mr Halcro.'

She was amused, making him feel lacking in acuity. 'Don't you know? I live there too.'

While he was trying to work that one out, searching for the right words, she strode over to the buggy and left him, waving a hand to him as she glided silently by and vanished lightless into the fog.

Another goddamned angle, he thought, almost with resignation. Was she Halcro's massively handsome live-in lover? His common-law wife? Possibly a wholly innocent lodger? He was left wondering whether or no he might last the night. There were moments when even that wasn't going to worry him whether he did or not.

# 21

During his interrogation of Kate Docherty, Rogers had noticed the arrival of Detective Inspector Coltart with his two accompanying DPCs and the force's Coroner's Officer. Now, while the two DPCs were helping to load Stoner's body into a coffin shell, he put Coltart in the picture about Stoner's death while conscious of an increasingly restless Halcro lowering at him for his attention.

The sea fog appeared to make the massive and phlegmatic Coltart even larger than life-size, a human version of an armoured vehicle; one who was a rabid non-smoker, a born-again teetotaller and a man not afraid to bend the ears of any senior officer being mistakenly within earshot with the details of his own, to them, uncivilized abstentions. He was also a misogynist, and one whose idea of current clothing fashion was an ill-fitting rust-brown suit generally accepted by his peers as having been run up by a drunken tent maker. Despite all this, he was no cheerless melancholic and Rogers liked him, even though he often questioned what on earth he had left to live for.

Rogers, taking thankfully the opportunity of leaning against the car in which Coltart had arrived, briefed the immediate future of the big detective and left him to use what troops he could muster at this ungodly hour to trace and interview those park employees who had been at large in the park, attending on the finding and recovery of Stoner's body, or had heard or seen anything of his death in the jaws of the tigress. 'The usual stuff,' Rogers said in the almost blandly optimistic manner of all executives in delegating those of their responsibilities which were the most tedious or soul-destroying.

Then, after being assured by Inspector Bragg that there had been no breaching of the enclosure's wire mesh fencing or any indication that Stoner may have climbed the unclimbable, he dismissed him back to his divisional duties with a hope that he might get more sleep that night than he, Rogers, had succeeded in getting.

The waiting Halcro wasn't exactly smouldering, though not too far from it. Rogers said placatingly, 'Sorry to have kept you, Mr Halcro, but I expect you know how it is when events are pushing you along,' though with this explanation the head keeper seemed not to agree at all.

'We were talking about security,' Rogers reminded him, trying not to give him any opening for venting his irritation. 'Inspector Bragg tells me there's been no break-in and no obvious climbing in either.'

'That's what I was going to tell you when you buggered off with Mrs Docherty. My chap had already done most of the checking against Stoner cutting his way in, or squeezing through some rat hole that doesn't exist anyway. And he hadn't. Neither can I think of any reason why the bloody fool should, seeing that as a guard he has access to the keys to all the personnel entry gates. Nor am I satisfied, if he hadn't got the key with him – and he wouldn't unless there was an emergency – that he would be able to scale the fence. God Almighty! The apertures in the mesh are diamond-shaped and not big enough to be able to put the toe of a normal-sized shoe in. And they'd be murder on your fingers if you tried to hand-climb it.' He looked as if he were about to savage the burning cheroot he held in his fingers.

'So he must have got in through the gate,' Rogers said. 'You found it unlocked?'

'I found it locked. What's more, I looked through his pockets for a key long before you arrived. He didn't have one and if he had I'd have told you.'

'It might have fallen out when he was being savaged, yes?' Rogers suggested. He had taken a surreptitious look at his wrist-watch, wondering where the hell Lingard could now be just when he was wanted. He was feeling an almost desperate need for a pipe of tobacco, then remembered dismally that he'd smoked the last of it and this in his present dog-weariness made him wonder whether or not he was cursed of the gods who seemed to be failing in their care for him. His tired brain was pushing him into that mood.

'It could've,' Halcro agreed. 'And if it did it'll stay there until daylight tomorrow.'

'He could have carried a key without authority? Or do the guards carry any of them as routine?'

'No, they don't. Any duplicate keys are kept on a key board in Mrs Wing's office and they're only for use in a serious emergency.' He scowled. 'It's to my certain knowledge that the bugger wasn't on duty this evening at all.' He pushed the cheroot back in his mouth with a sort of finality.

'So whatever the circumstances, the gate had been locked after he'd gone through it?'

'Yes,' Halcro answered around the cheroot, the smoke from it almost attractively acrid in Rogers's starved nose.

'It'd be odd then if he'd locked it behind himself, wouldn't it? Even taking the unlikely view that he may have been contemplating suicide, it wouldn't be logical for him to have cared a damn whether it was locked or unlocked; or even to have hung on to the key?'

Halcro shrugged morosely. 'Don't ask me. I'm not a bloody detective.'

'No, you're not,' Rogers agreed amiably enough, pausing for a moment while one of the tigers, still unseen in the fog, was letting off some growling unhappiness. 'But you obviously knew Stoner. Would you think him the type to commit suicide in this bizarre manner? Or even commit it by some more usual means?'

'Hell, no,' Halcro growled. 'Not in a million years.'

'Are you thinking he's unlikely to have gone in there under his own steam?'

Halcro's forehead furrowed. 'Of course I am. Why would he?'

158

'I don't know,' the detective prevaricated. 'But then I'm a man of uncomplicated thinking.' He was nothing of the sort, though he sometimes thought he might be. 'So how did you get him out without getting yourself chewed up?'

Halcro was patient with him for a change. 'Don't be foolish, man. First of all we're friendly with both Lalapur and Rajah to the extent that we treat them like the oversized cats they are. Mind, the knowing is always there that they can wop you a dangerous one in a fit of irritation, or even in play, just as a domestic cat can. We've known them for years, though that doesn't mean we're fireproof in a manner of speaking, but almost so. Still, when there *is* trouble we're required to go in armed with a gun and a high-powered spray – it's a harmless pacifying spray, that's all, but it's very uncomfortable to have done to you – and pray to God we don't have to use either. In this event there was never a suggestion that we'd need to do anything but to tell them both to bugger off – which they did. That left us to collect Stoner who was dead by then anyway.'

'Wouldn't you use an anaesthetizing dart pistol like the one Mr Latouche has? He was here, so Inspector Bragg told me.'

'He'd heard the noise – how couldn't he when the siren was being blasted off – and came running, bringing his pistol case with him. He knew when he got here that it was no occasion for laying out either of the tigers and I wouldn't have let him anyway. They're my animals and my responsibility and with Stoner dead it would only be a matter of pacifying them at the worst and that wasn't necessary anyway. I told him so when he arrived.'

'Didn't he go all professional on you at that?'

Halcro showed his surprise. 'What? Jacques? Never. He couldn't pull rank on me anyway and he's never wanted to.'

'I can understand that.' Rogers was unable to make that less than caustic, though he thought rather undeservedly so. More genially, he said, 'I do have to see Mr Latouche and I know he lives in the castle, though not exactly where.'

'The third floor up, which is the top one. It overlooks his clinic at the back.' He flipped his burned-out cheroot into the road. 'You've finished with me?' he asked, sounding not too displeased at the prospect of it.

'Thank you for your time, Mr Halcro,' Rogers said. Had there been a more affable meeting of minds between them he might, in his deprivation, have asked him for one of his cheroots, evil-smelling though the smoke was to even his palate.

Leaving the morose head keeper for the solitude of some serious thinking, he walked slowly through the undiminishing fog – where things still loomed – towards the castle, hoping not to fall on his face *en route*. He had in him the need to resort to his inner consciousness in contemplating matters such as Stoner's guilt, the single gunshot heard during the night of the murder and any probable access to Latouche's anaesthetizing pistol by an outside agency.

## 22

*En route* for his interview with Latouche Rogers thought, not too seriously though certainly in a mind mostly shrouded in sleep's shadow, that there should be a law – divine or secular, he didn't mind which – against inflicting more than three murders in one stretch of twenty-four hours on any single suffering investigating officer. Stoner was without doubt the unneeded fourth and that he was hoping to discuss with Latouche who could be, it seemed, the repository of an answer or two.

Entering the castle's inner courtyard through the tunnel with the prospect of a three-floor climb to Latouche's apartment, he saw through the obscuring darkness, which appeared to him to resemble a Jack the Ripper London fog, the dim glow of diffused light showing from between the slats of a venetian blind; almost certainly indicating the veterinarian's late working.

Standing not much further than the thickness of a coat of

paint from the clinic's door, he listened at it to confirm or not its occupancy by Latouche, hearing almost inaudible sounds of documents being slapped down and, once, what seemed to be the slow and cautious opening of a metal filing drawer.

Satisfied, but unable to find a bell push, he knocked on the door, a sudden authoritative bare-knuckle rapping in the quietness of the night. When there was no reply – a significance of apprehension to Rogers's waiting acuity – he knocked again, more peremptorily this time.

It was Latouche who answered from inside with a 'Yes? What is it?' in a distinctly unwelcoming voice.

'Superintendent Rogers here, Mr Latouche,' the detective identified himself – it could be the voice of doom for him, he thought. 'I'd like urgent words with you about Stoner's death.'

There were a few seconds of small noises of what Rogers took to be a furtive and hurried removal of unidentifiable things before the door was opened and Latouche appeared, a darkly amorphous figure against a brightly lit interior. Even so, Rogers sensed a keyed-up tautness about him.

'May I come in?' He stepped forward, obliging Latouche to open wider the door.

'I'm sorry,' Latouche said. 'I'm so busy . . . couldn't it wait for tomorrow?'

'An investigation into someone's death waits for no man, I'm afraid,' Rogers told him tritely, brooking no refusal by being already in. 'I shouldn't keep you long.'

'Come in.' Latouche sounded definitely unhappy. In the brightness of the inside lights Rogers could see that he was even more haggard and hollow-eyed, more apprehensive, than when he had seen him earlier that evening; an evening which seemed to be farther away than a mere six hours. He still wore his elegant off-white suit – a little grubby at the edges now, and creased – with the sand-coloured shirt and yellow tie, and the handkerchief flopping from the breast pocket.

Inviting the detective to sit, he sat himself at the desk which had been denuded of the row of textbooks Rogers had seen on it earlier, though everything else on it had been left. He also saw what appeared to be the end of a blue fabric holdall on the floor behind the desk. It seemed to Rogers that something calamitous had hit Latouche and this was a happening he was prepared to exploit.

He gave him an encouraging smile. 'I'll soon be out of your way,' he said, ignoring the signs of what he thought to be an apparently unannounced departure. 'It's that I'm rather baffled by the circumstances of Stoner's death in the tigers' enclosure.' His forehead creased his supposed bafflement. 'Why would he be in there anyway? Am I to accept that there is evidence of his need to dine with panthers, so to speak?'

Latouche was nodding his agreement. 'Yes, why not? It's my opinion exactly, and I'm unable to come up with a more likely reason. It's been done by the deranged at other parks and zoos, though so far specifically with lions. You have to consider too that Stoner was undoubtedly a short generation or two from an ancestral primitive and as such probably unaccountable in his emotions by our standards. I could believe anything bizarre from him.'

Having said that into Rogers's silence, he added, 'He wouldn't be the first – nor the last either – to deliberately enter a big cat's enclosure to search out a weird kind of death.'

Rogers nodded amiably enough as if there was something in what Latouche was saying. 'But there is an alternative,' he pointed out. 'He could have been something of a nuisance – a dangerous nuisance to somebody. A somebody who either tricked him by some means into going in as a conscientious security guard and then locked him in there with no escape; or possibly, put him in when he was in no condition to object.'

He was staring blandly at Latouche's uninformative face from which he plainly would not receive too much help. 'I was wondering . . .' he said, shaking his head as if in frustration. 'Possibly . . . no, perhaps not.' He bit at his bottom lip, then appeared to push himself into saying, 'I was going to ask you about the safekeeping of the anaesthetizing pistol you told me about. And the suspected breaking into this clinic that you mentioned . . .'

162

He tailed off, primarily because he wished to leave his words hanging in an atmosphere of growing tenseness, but partly also because he thought he had heard quiet, seemingly subterranean, sounds of movement from behind the inner door at the back of him. It took some self-discipline not to show his awareness of it by his expression or any turning of his head.

'The pistol's been held in perfectly adequate safekeeping,' Latouche said stiffly. 'I took it to the enclosure when I heard the siren and I think that Harry Halcro will have told you so.'

He reached into a drawer of his desk which had patently been already open and took out the pistol itself, placing it gently on to the green leather surface of the desk with its muzzle pointing more or less in Rogers's direction. 'Is this what you mean?' he asked.

Whether used primarily for anaesthetizing or tranquillizing an animal or not, it was a dangerous-looking weapon. It had a long and thin blue-black barrel attached by a knurled nut to a bulky blond-wood butt for fingers to clutch to, and with the trigger mechanism of an orthodox gun.

'I'd be grateful', Rogers said carefully, 'if, loaded or unloaded, you'd not leave it pointing in my direction.' He essayed a stiff smile. 'It's one of my minor phobias, I'm afraid, against having a gun of any kind seemingly aimed at me.' His sweat glands were playing him up for he could feel a warm dampness on his back.

'I'm sorry,' Latouche said thickly, somehow not quite with it and holding Rogers in his gaze while pulling it back an inch or two though leaving it still pointing in the detective's direction. 'I'd left it loaded, but it's safe enough for the time being.' The veterinary was now looking far from stable, his expression fraught.

For Rogers, if not for Latouche, the cards were on the table and he had first to play those which might bring in the highest return. He was in no doubt now that the pistol was being used as a weapon. He stared hard at Latouche's uninformative face from which he saw plainly he would receive little help, and changed course.

'You've heard, I'm sure, about young Coope's murder and his being found in Stoner's cottage?' he said carefully, keeping his apparent amiability on show and at the same time trying to keep track of the occasionally stealthy sounds coming from behind the inner door.

'Yes. A terrible ending for so nice a lad.' There had been a hard brought-out concern for Coope in his voice. 'That was unforgivable.'

'And you wouldn't be surprised at my telling you that there's no doubt about Stoner's having done it? That he killed Coope, I mean.'

'No. Not if you're telling me.'

'That's what I'm doing. Also that Stoner seems to be the man responsible for the murders of your Harriet and Henry Fowler. You wouldn't dispute that, would you?'

Latouche swallowed audibly and, for a moment, looked dreadfully vulnerable. 'No. It's of a piece with how I thought it to be.' The long slender fingers of his unoccupied hand were tapping lightly on the desk's surface.

'Your Harriet for whom you had a great affection, yes?'

'Indeed. As . . . as I told you.'

'What actually was there between Stoner and Harriet that caused you to hate him?'

For a brief moment Latouche looked as if Rogers had hit him. 'Please don't push at that,' he said miserably. 'I won't have her made dirty any further.'

'I'm sorry, I won't,' Rogers promised. 'But you do accept that Stoner shot Fowler in the summerhouse and then killed Harriet?'

'I must, mustn't I,' he said with the glimmer of unshed tears in his eyes. Then he added violently, 'He was a brute; a filthy brute, and he deserved to die.'

'So he might, but let's see if he was the only one; the only one implicated in the shooting.' Rogers had hardened his voice almost to the accusatorial. 'The shot that killed Fowler was the only shot heard last night. Did you know that then?'

There was an uneasy silence in which Rogers could hear in

the quietness of the ticking of his own wrist-watch from under his shirt cuff and Latouche's quickened breathing.

'No, I didn't,' Latouche got out at last. 'Was it?'

'You know it was.' Rogers was grim-faced, contempt in his voice. 'You gave that so-called filthy brute – your words – an alibi for the two murders – one of them of your Harriet – in claiming that he was with you when you both heard the sound of the gun being fired. There was enough in that one act to implicate you into being an accessory to the murders. What's your answer to that, Mr Latouche?'

During Rogers's accusation, an apparently shrunken Latouche had glanced at the pistol still close to his hand while the detective felt the chill of imagining the other's intent to use it. With that, and the knowledge that there was somebody active elsewhere in the clinic, there was little comfort there for him.

'No,' Latouche said, not very convincingly. 'You haven't got it right.'

'My theory is this,' Rogers continued as if he hadn't heard his denial. 'Stoner was set up to kill Fowler for reasons which are probably apparent to you, if not to me. I might concede that he killed Harriet for some reason of his own or to conceal what he'd done to Fowler, but so be it. When he spoke to you on your return to the park – that is, if he actually did – it was no doubt by an earlier arrangement to provide him with an alibi. To give you some credit which you might not deserve – and I could be over-generous in this – it's possible that you were then unaware that he had killed Mrs Stoner as well as Fowler.'

Latouche had shaken his head blindly as he listened to this, though not so blindly that he was forgetting about the pistol still pointing at the detective. Rogers knew then that although he had hit sensitive guilty flesh with his words, they weren't getting him anywhere.

'Let me go on,' Rogers said with unremitting sternness. 'I believe that someone bigger and more important than you had been protecting Stoner and the word came down – or it already existed – that he wasn't accountable to you and

165

wasn't to be touched in what he did. This would put a stopper on any thoughts you might have of administering too obviously your own version of justice on him for the killing of Harriet, for whom you've agreed you had a deep affection.'

He paused, believing he could read in Latouche's face what he had been looking for. 'I see', he said, less sternly, 'that I might be making some sense to you.'

'Go on,' the distressed-looking veterinarian almost whispered, 'though I'm not agreeing with you.'

'I believe you discharged whatever obligation you felt you were under to Mrs Stoner by having the tigers do it for you.' He nodded at the pistol resting so near to Latouche's hand. 'With the help of that thing to give Stoner no chance of objecting.' He had a brief glimpse in his mind of the bloody-jawed tigress playing with a drugged Stoner as a cat might with a mouse.

There was silence for several moments with Latouche's sad eyes never leaving his, for all animosity seemed to have left him.

'I'm convinced', Rogers continued, 'that, for whatever reason, you and possibly another person shot and anaesthetized Stoner and left him locked in the tigers' enclosure, knowing that a tigress with cubs would almost certainly finish him off without any further help from you. And if she hadn't? Who was he to complain to anyone without dropping himself into the possibility of a multiple murder charge?'

Latouche took that rather well for a man who had anyway started the interview with an apprehension of doom written in his face. 'You would have great difficulty in proving any of that, even were your facts right,' he said, too confidently for Rogers's satisfaction. He grimaced at the pistol, Rogers not sure of that as a good sign or bad. 'Stoner', Latouche said, 'deserved to die. Whoever did it, whoever persuaded him into entering the enclosure, was doing society – civilization if you like – a good turn. You might say it was left to a higher authority whether he should die or not.' For those few moments of speech, his sad eyes held in them the irrational stare of zealotry.

Rogers had had enough and he heaved his tired body upright. 'My higher authority is the law,' he said brusquely. 'I'm sorry, but I'm taking you into custody on suspicion of having been concerned in the murder of William Stoner and . . .'

He had stopped when Latouche had, without a change of expression, picked up the pistol, wrapping his pale and not too aggressive fist around its butt and pointing it at his chest which suddenly felt full of pounding heart.

He thought that while he was now by way of being nervous about that bloody pistol being waved at him, Latouche was probably frightened too; undoubtedly scared about something other than what he'd done about feeding Stoner to the tigers. And a scared man with a pistol in his hand was doubly dangerous.

'Please sit,' Latouche ordered him. 'I'm afraid you'll have to stay here.'

Rogers, deciding he could sit without appearing to be frightened into doing so, said, 'You're threatening me? I just want to be sure that you know exactly what you're doing.' Anything to keep him talking, he felt.

Latouche was unhappy again. 'It isn't like that, but you mustn't leave. Not yet.' He lowered his voice, looking over Rogers's shoulder. 'I had no reason to suppose that Stoner would do what he did, certainly not with Harriet. It was against everything we'd want anyway. That he killed poor Coope worsened it. He had to go, even though he was Toby Wimbush's own appointee, and certainly whatever was to happen wasn't remotely in my remit.'

Rogers heard again the soft sounds of movement from behind the inner door and it worried him. 'There's somebody here with you,' he said, feeling now a kind of fatalism and at the same time judging whether in his present state he could suddenly push the manifestly heavy desk into Latouche's belly before his finger could squeeze at the trigger of the menacing pistol.

'Yes, there is,' Latouche agreed, 'and I'm sorry about it.' Suddenly authoritative, he called out loudly, *'Charles! Come in, please!'*

Rogers, instinctively turning his head at the sound of the opening door, saw momentarily a tall thin-faced man with dark brown wavy hair and wearing opaque Mafia-style sun spectacles on a long nose, whom he immediately noticed to be an empty-handed though decidedly aggressive-looking character wearing a light-coloured summer jacket, narrow white trousers and an open-necked shirt. As he turned back to Latouche, seconds too late to do anything sensible with the desk, so the voice yelled from the back of him, *'For Christ's sake, you stupid bastard . . . do it! Do it now!'* then hearing the frightening crack of the pistol being fired and feeling a shocking blow in his left arm and the knowledge coming subliminally that he might be going to die as a tiger's dinner in just the same way as had Stoner. Then there was a rising fury as he tried to lift himself from his chair and feeling an arm hard around his throat, seeing hanging on his own arm a thin aluminium tube with red feather flights at its end; and oh! Christ! it was now hurting him and he was going to die, shouting in his aggression as he struggled to push the immovable desk at this bastard Latouche now standing with pistol pointing at his chest and saying something about being dreadfully sorry only he couldn't hear clearly because the bastard whose arm was choking him was yelling about this bloody son of a bitch he couldn't hold for much bloody longer and the smell of whisky from him that he only recognized above the pain in his arm and the wooziness and the beginning of a vomit as a darkness was creeping across his vision and drifting him into a limp feebleness, his nose and mouth somehow squashed against the hard surface of the desk in the despair of his coming plunge into the darkness that was overtaking him . . .

# 23

It had come as something of a surprise for Rogers to wake from what had been a dreamless unconsciousness to find himself in a hospital bed with his wrist attached by a tube to a spindly chromium-plated stand – one of several menacing-looking machines grouped around the head of his bed – which held a polythene bag of what appeared to his ceiling-wards stare to be crystal-clear water. Moreover, he was wearing somebody's too-small blue pyjamas marked with the upside-down words 'Property of the National Health Service' and long white woollen stockings. His arm hurt ferociously, he had a thumping headache and he felt that at any moment he would bring up.

A white-faced clock on an opposite white wall had told him it was 3.25 in the afternoon, and the afternoon only because he had been sufficiently *compos mentis* to detect sunlight behind the closed window curtains. He had assumed then that he was in a private room at the Abbotsburn Royal United Hospital and that he might be going to live.

Having with difficulty pressed the bell-tit on the wall above his head – there was a name-card by its side with 'Dr A. Stasher' printed on it – he had been visited by a nurse and then in turn by two doctors. One was a bouncy little blonde of undoubted efficiency with a Mid-European accent and a penchant for breathing gently on his flesh and touching him with exciting searching fingers as she examined the different aspects of his body in which she was interested; and he wasn't that ill that he didn't appreciate it. The other, a lugubrious medical humorist who was probably Stasher, told Rogers from a straight blue-jowled face that even for an apparently criminally careless policeman – who had obviously been mistaken for one of the larger apes – he was lucky to be still more or less alive. The dart which had been fired at him, he was told, apart from containing a dosage designed for an animal heavier than himself, had also had a faulty anti-penetration flange and had in consequence penetrated too far into his arm, hitting the cephalic vein and chipping his arm bone; this, it was implied, had not been a good thing to happen at all.

The nurses were, of course, wonderful and in the five hours since waking up he had proposed marriage to three of them –

all at once if they wished, he had said – and had been accepted in the same vein in which his proposals had been made. In doing this he had felt that he had it in him to recover.

Lingard, his first permitted visitor, was shown into the room after daylight's reddish glow had fled from the now pulled-back window curtains. His second-in-command showed very little of his usual debonair manner. He looked tired, unshaven and unscrubbed; his once immaculate suit suffered from what could only be called a godawful grubbiness in Lingard's own language. Life obviously hadn't been all that good to him during the past few hours, though his humour had remained intact.

'How d'you feel, George?' he greeted him.

Propped up on five pillows, Rogers said, 'I think I've felt better, and you'll not inherit my chair just yet. You're suffering?'

'I should be.' He sat himself at the foot of the bed. 'I've had Pitt-Bowsher on my tail about what happened to you – a degree of carelessness on your part he seemed to think – and a Chief Superintendent Gamble from the Regional Crime Squad making a bloody nuisance of himself about the detective sergeant he says he planted in the park.' He cocked a quizzical eyebrow. 'Were you holding out on me, George? Not to be trusted with a piddling little drugs smash?'

'Not my choice, David. Confidentiality was wrung from me. No exceptions, no whisper of who Fowler actually was and what he was supposed to be doing.' When he saw that Lingard was accepting that, he said, 'So now you're here to tell me what the score was after I'd been put down?'

'More precisely, I've been ordered to find out what it was before you were anaesthetized near unto death in the late Latouche's clinic . . .'

'The late Latouche!' Rogers interrupted him, wondering what the hell.

'Yes, death has snatched him from under our noses, I'm afraid.' Lingard wasn't to be pushed. 'Let me tell it as it happened.'

'But he is dead?' Rogers felt curiously deflated.

'Yes, and you yourself had a close call with the life eternal or whatever according to authoritative medical opinion. When I came back to the park with Lesley – it was touching on midnight – and we were trying to find our way in the fog, we saw Latouche had a light showing from his clinic; which, Lesley said, was terribly unusual for that time of the night. I banged on the door for a bit and getting nothing for it, then tottered up the castle steps to where Lesley said he had his apartment. It was in darkness and if he was in there then he wasn't answering my ringing so we knew something was going on, and something especially worrying to Lesley who liked the cove.'

He took out from a pocket his small ivory box and pinched and inhaled a self-indulgent ration of snuff from it. 'That's better,' he said. 'It clears the sinuses. A very worried Lesley', he continued, 'fetched a duplicate key from her office and there you were in the clinic snoring with your face most off-puttingly resting on the vet's desk where you'd puked, dead to the wide with a dart stuck in your arm. While I did my stuff in looking for Latouche and finding his car missing, Lesley – sweet girl – was blubbing about your condition – she thought you were on the verge, given a missing pulse or two – while ringing emergency for an ambulance.'

He was brooding for a moment or two, taking in Rogers's unhappy condition. 'You were definitely next door to being no longer with us, if you get my meaning.' He paused, then said solicitously, 'You can stand all this, George? You look a bit sick about it.'

'I can if it doesn't take too long, and I'm sorry I spoiled your evening with Lesley.' He said it without rancour, having buried any thoughts tending towards lechery with her.

'No problem,' Lingard told him cheerfully. 'There'll be other times when you won't be needing our personal and urgent attention. That is, I hope not.'

'Carry on then, David. Somehow I've to remember that you're talking about me and not some other poor buggered-up victim.'

'Yes, you have,' Lingard acknowledged, anxious to finish,

for Lesley was waiting to see him later that evening, yet cautious of appearing obvious about it. 'By the time we reached Casualty, the medico on duty didn't then know what the stuff was that you'd had injected in you, other than whatever it was it wasn't the sort to be administered by a dart even to a hard-nosed fella like you. I had to leave you pro tem in the hospital's tender loving care so that I could get back to the park and find out where Latouche was and what the blazes was going on where it was thought necessary by somebody to lay impious hands on yourself. Well, he definitely hadn't returned to either the clinic or his apartment, and it was evident that he'd flown the coop. So in almost total ignorance of what was going on I put out a wanted circulation for an arrestable offence I wasn't even certain about.'

'I could have shot the dart at myself, of course,' Rogers said sardonically.

'I should have thought of that,' Lingard said in mock regret, then putting aside his flippancy, said, 'For good or whatever, the chasing around after him was for nothing. I'm afraid the poor devil had already bought it in the most horrific way you can imagine. At daybreak this morning his body was found on the east shoulder of Morte Moor having fallen or been pushed from an aircraft.'

Lingard's face showed his revulsion. 'I saw the poor sod. He had burst open like a paper sack of water and was only held together by his suit; not a sight for the faint-hearted. There were reports, too, that a chopper was flying over Pauncey Chetford village after midnight last night and near to where he was found. The two incidents would seem to tie together.'

'A syndicate pick-up and a closing of accounts?' Rogers suggested. 'Thank God I haven't got it on my plate.'

'We'll miss you, George,' Lingard said drily. 'Wilfred did a quick check on what we'd finally put together of Latouche and he said no problem; he'd accept that he had fallen from an aircraft at least five-hundred feet above the moor. He's had them before when parachutes have failed to open.' He flipped open his tiny box again, inhaling a generous pinch of snuff in each nostril. 'How say you, George?'

172

'It's extraordinary, and I'm damned sorry.' Rogers meant it, too, in an odd sort of way. 'I approved of him and his old-fashioned morality. I can't believe he was nearly so evil as the chap who pushed him out of the chopper.'

'You're thinking it was Laurence Stoner, of course?'

'Yes, I am. Even though Latouche called him Charles. I recollected then that he had used the name as an alias. And then there was your description of him. How did you know?'

'Magnus found his fingerprints down in the cellar where they had been clearing out a small laboratory of sorts. God knows how often he was able to visit Latouche, or how he could work with him from the prison.'

'Careless, though, wasn't he, for a man with his record and a dangerous habit of spending time away from Hardenhuish.' Rogers remained silent for a short space of time as if in an inner contemplation of things, then said, 'Back to Fowler before I lose what I was going to say. Now that you've got all this on your plate, I should point out that he almost certainly hadn't been exposed as a plant. It'd be difficult to believe that Latouche or Laurence Stoner wouldn't have pulled out immediately; not waited until a load of CID arrived and started asking questions. That should give Gamble some comfort; some embarrassment too, to know poor old Fowler was having it off with a woman who could well have been involved in the drugs business.'

'All noted and agreed.' Lingard had been watching Rogers closely. 'You're looking a mite bushed, George, and I shouldn't be long in going.'

'And talking of going, I didn't go gently, you know.' Rogers had his pride and he wasn't to be thought of as being something like a poor slaughtered sheep. 'It took the two of them, with Stoner coming up behind me.' He recounted his ill-chosen decision to visit the clinic on his own and what had happened in there. Then he said, 'I'm tired, David, and bloody sick of it all and I need to make up on my sleep. Perhaps you'll come again tomorrow? Take my chair over for the next couple of days and clear up some of the paperwork, would you?'

'It'll be my pleasure, George, but don't collapse on me just yet. I'll be as quick as I can, but Pitt-Bowsher wants – demands, I should say – a few specifics from your suffering condition. Firstly, do you really believe that Mrs Stoner was actually involved?'

'Either she was or she had found out about the set-up involving Latouche. She was his secretary and would have been dim-witted not to have suspected something was going on. What I am sure about is that she never suspected that her so-called husband was concerned in anything with Latouche, and Latouche himself was at pains to express his dislike of him. I don't think we'll ever know the answer to that and I'm not sure that it matters that we don't. Let the Coroner work it out for himself if anything touching on it is brought out at the inquest.'

'What about the brutish Stoner?'

'He must have been involved in some aspect of it to have Latouche stand in with an alibi for him. Being dead is his answer to anything we may want to do about it.'

'And Coope? I've a change of mind about him.'

'So have I, David. I think it reasonable to suppose that the poor bugger was spotted by Stoner who then supposed that he could have been seen himself at the summerhouse. It wouldn't take much for a frightened and desperate Stoner to entice Coope into visiting him at his house, there to be silenced while Stoner himself went under cover.' He yawned prodigiously. 'Is that it?' he asked pointedly.

'That's it,' Lingard said cheerfully, 'and it didn't kill you, did it?'

'Only just short of it.' Rogers lowered his voice. 'You'll find a key to my apartment in my trousers pocket, wherever they may be. There's a pipe, tobacco and matches on the table by my bed. You'll be doing me a favour if you'll have them collected and brought here later this evening. Not advertising them, naturally. A policewoman?' he suggested. 'They have clutch bags and who'd suspect?'

'Egad, George, but you're a wicked bastard,' Lingard said, rising and turning to go, then saying, 'Ah! I nearly forgot.

A letter from Angharad that she's anxious you should get.' He withdrew a white envelope from his pocket and dropped it at Rogers's side, smiling not without sympathy for him and leaving him to his privacy as he picked it up.

Rogers, holding the letter, was deeply pessimistic about it, believing that it must surely amount to his dismissal in favour of the well-heeled Sir Charles in whom Angharad surely must have something other than an intellectual and physical interest; possibly his yacht, his city chambers, his legal eminence, his knighthood and his bloody MBE awarded for sitting on a coat-of-arms-decorated seat and pontificating on civil law.

He thought he could almost read her scrawling writing through the envelope he couldn't bring himself to open, believing he would see something like 'My dear George, I am finding this a most difficult letter to write . . . I regret my decision which will probably make us both unhappy . . . I feel it best for both of us . . .' His mind shied away from its contemplation and they were long minutes before he decided that, like life after death, there must be something after a lost love and that he had better get it over with.

Ripping the envelope open, he withdrew the folded cream-laid paper, forcing himself to read it.

*George dear. You need looking after like a great big baby and I don't feel that my projected future as a sort of female aide-mémoire for Charles fits well with my worrying about you. If this makes you feel like an auctioneer's lot number, then so be it, for I need you. I am told that you were careless enough to allow yourself to be shot with a tranquillizing gun, whatever that is, and you probably needed it. Necessarily with much affection. Angharad.*

With his present gloom giving way to a beaming smile, he wondered how soon he could get himself discharged, for it couldn't be said that he was still in a life-threatening condition. Not when his body felt like this about the lovely and so desirable Angharad Rhys Pritchard, naval officer's widow and barrister-at-law in waiting.

Now waiting for him, and not for an unfortunate Sir Charles for whom he could now feel pity.